MAGIC FOR A RAINY DAY

PUBLISHED BY TANGLED SKY PRESS

Visit our website: www.tangledskypress.com

This is an original publication of Tangled Sky Press.

First edition: March 2017

PRINTED IN THE UNITED STATES OF AMERICA

MAGIC FOR A RAINY DAY

FIVE CONTEMPORARY FAIRY STORIES

ALEXANDRA BRANDT

TANGLED SKY PRESS

www.TangledSkyPress.com

For Nannette, my very first fan

INTRODUCTION

I suppose you could say the theme of *Magic for a Rainy Day* is Celtic fairy lore-inspired contemporary fantasy stories. Or maybe the theme is light, happy-ending stories set in rainy locations (like the Pacific Northwest, Ireland, and Scotland).

Or all of the above...but really, this collection is for my mother. That's the theme. Stories that Nannette enjoys (including some that I wrote specifically to make her happy).

Why? I have her to thank for my lifelong obsession with books: she was my introduction to the joys of genre fiction, from the Brother Cadfael murder mysteries to Regency romances to Anne McCaffrey's dragons and Ursula K. LeGuin. My love for all things Speculative Fiction — and thus my profound (and proud) geekery — can be traced back to her.

She was also my first cheerleader.

An eminently practical woman herself (a genius doctor and a highly effective and organized human in general), she still loves the arts, and always encouraged me to follow what I loved most. You see, ever since I could pick up a book, I had decided I was going to be a writer. Through the years, I don't ever remember my mother telling me I needed to focus on getting a 'real' career, even when I decided to major in English...and switch my minor from archaeology to art... to German...to history...

(Strangely enough — and I have her to thank for this as well — I managed to actually get a day job that used my writing and artistic skills, but we had no idea I would be so lucky.)

But most importantly, my mother's eagerness to read my stories was one of the key factors in deciding to stop thinking about writing and actually do it.

I got the idea to create this collection for her because of one story in particular: "Banoffee Pie and Black Pudding." It was one of the first stories I wrote when I 'got serious' about writing in 2010 (i.e. actually started finishing stories that I started, instead of leaving them to slowly expire in my documents folder). It was just a light, fluffy thing — I thought — that I'd written furiously over the course of a few days for a writing workshop.

My mother loved it.

Genuinely, not just because I was her daughter and she had to love my work. I know this because she still talks about it years later.

I've been writing darker stories recently, and I think she's a bit wistful for the light, happy-ending days of yore.

So I've gathered my happiest stories — from both those 'days of yore' and more recent — and even written a few more just for this collection. As you'll discover, the Celtic flavor, and especially the Scottish connection, all comes from my mother too. (I've been very, very lucky to take many wonderful, eye-opening trips with my family to the places we love.)

Ultimately, my successful genius doctor mother loves fiction because it's her escape. And frankly, I sometimes need that escape too.

So I guess this collection is for both of us.

I hope it brings you joy, Mom.

Alexandra Brandt
December 2016

The author and her mother, about to go Scottish Country Dancing. Because that's the kind of nerdy they embrace.

SIDEWYND

Here begins my love affair with Scotland, for which I most certainly have my mother to thank. In 2015, I had the amazing privilege of going on a three-week tour of Scotland's incredible archaeology with my husband and parents. It was everything my heart could want — ancient things, mysterious and beautiful and spooky.

It sparked many ideas for stories, as I knew it would, but I didn't realize the city of Edinburgh itself would inspire a little urban fantasy series about the Royal Mile, with all of its named alleys (wynds, closes, and courts), just waiting to be explored. Just begging to be turned into something magical.

Sky Patel stood with her oldest friend under the arch of Borthwick's Close and knew things were drawing to an end at last.

She leaned against the wall, hands in the pockets of her faded summer-weight anorak. The old alley's cold musty smell of damp stone, the uneven paving under her feet, the rough surface of the crumbling old walls all seemed sharper, clearer, more significant today. The sounds of the crowds of Edinburgh tourists, street performers, and motor vehicles on the Royal Mile seemed so distant, for all they were just outside the entryway.

His hand on her shoulder, Ramsay gestured in the other direction, down the narrow alley. "Shall you do the honors, my dear?"

Sky shook her head mutely. She was as adept at opening a Sideway as any Wyndling, but this was too much to ask today. The familiar hum of ancient power that lay in the roots of the city, in the stones of these close walls, didn't seem particularly comforting this time.

Ram seemed to understand. "Ah well, once more for old time's sake, then. My last Sideway."

Sky's eyes stung. She blinked rapidly to clear them as she began to follow him further in. A grown woman — especially one of her age — had no business crying over her best friend's retirement. And yet…

"Wait," she found herself saying. "Just let me…look at you a minute." He smiled and paused mid-stride, turning. He patiently allowed her to finish drinking in the details of his worn old form, with its well-used crown of white curls, the wire-rimmed glasses hiding sharp earth-brown eyes, the stooped posture and gnarled hands. He still insisted on wearing a kilt every day, a bit unusual for this day and age, but on him it seemed charmingly eccentric. Oh, she would miss this version of Ramsay Whitebridge.

But she couldn't stall any longer. Her resigned expression must have said it all, for Ram nodded once, his eyes kind, and began the gesture to draw on the deep, slow power within the medieval bones of Borthwick's Close's walls, to pull and shape it into the opening that would bring them to the Sidewynd. No one on the street noticed, of course. They never did.

Then the two of them stepped through, and transformed.

The close itself remained a winding little tunnel-like alley of crumbling stone, but everything else changed in an instant. The sounds of motorists and babbling tourists and street performers were gone, replaced by the chatter of voices that weren't human, the sound of faint music coming from somewhere, the tinkle and rustle and patter of beings of all shapes and sizes moving just beyond the archway.

Ram stood six inches taller than Sky now, his shock of white curls longer, wilder. Great, curling horns now framed his face, which had elongated and changed shape to resemble a goat or a sheep more than a man. His legs had changed shape too, now covered in white woolly curls beneath his kilt, although his feet more resembled a gargoyle's than hooves of a goat.

It never ceased to amaze her, that her friend could conceal all of that beneath the form of an eccentric old man. But Ram had always been very good at illusions, what folks on the other side would call "fairy glamour." Not that he would need to use it again.

Sky was lucky that she required so little glamour of her own to blend in with the humans, and still it was always with some relief that she dropped all illusions in the Wynd. Sky's warm brown skin and features of a pretty fortyish East Indian woman remained the same, but her ears were now oddly-shaped and tipped with golden-brown fur. A slender tail swished below the hem of her anorak, likewise shading to deep, soft gold and ending with a plume-like tuft of fur. Her eyes had changed from light brown to bright blue – not an abnormal human color, but so vivid in her brown face as to be a bit too noticeable on the streets. Summer Sky Blue, her own true self.

She faced Ram — Old White, as he was known on the Wynd side — and looked him up and down again. "Are you sure you want to do this? Leave Edinburgh, leave humanity's side of the city for good?"

He rumbled a laugh, and gestured for her to follow him onto the Spine, the Wyndside version of the Royal Mile. They had a purpose here, and he was becoming wise to her stalling tactics.

"My retirement is long overdue, dear Sky Blue," he reminded her as they dodged a swarm of whirring creatures in the balmy air and turned right to go down the steep hill.

The Spine echoed the shape and length of its human equivalent, although the buildings along either side didn't seem to follow the laws of physics in any way. Nor, for that matter, did the Spine itself. Time to get from one place to another always seemed to vary wildly. Everywhere here the colors were unnaturally bright, and the sounds and smells seemed to have their own shape and texture. Sky remembered well the feeling of wild disorientation and delighted wonder that had accompanied her first sojourn into the Sidewynd. These days, she preferred the experience in small doses, and it was always better with Old White at her side. How would she manage in the future?

She linked her slender arm with her friend's woolly one, muttering something about it all being far too soon. Surely he had years yet.

Ram put his hand on her arm and squeezed, but continued to gently propel them down the street. "Now, now. I've put in my three hundred years and seen the face of that city change beyond anything we could have imagined. I'm looking forward to finding a corner of the Wynd to settle in. Maybe I'll raise a family at last. Surely you can't deny me that?" His eyes twinkled.

There wasn't a good argument in response to that. Of course he was allowed his happiness. And the city wouldn't go unprotected—some other powerful Wyndling, equally qualified, would take his place as Protector soon enough.

They were at their destination now, a white building, deceptively small and plain. Wynd Law, read a severe black sign by the door. Three symbols accompanied the text: Wyndling name-stamps of the lawyers within.

"Come on, then," Ram said, and ushered her in the door.

⇌

When they emerged some hours later, the finality of Old White's retirement had finally sunk in. Ram had bequeathed to Sky all the tools of his position, despite her protests. Whatever new Protector came to Edinburgh would have his or her (or its) own tools, he'd explained. Who else deserved the Far-Seeing Eye, the Universal Map, and the assorted amulets of protection, but the woman who loved the city even more than he?

More importantly for Sky, they were pieces of Ram, and therefore she accepted them without too much argument. Well, no more than an hour's worth, anyway.

Now they stood again in Borthwick's Close, Wyndside. She now had a large gunnysack (illogically roomy on the inside, of course) that contained the tools and a heavy stack of papers bound by Wynd magic. With those, no Wyndlings could contest her claim to Ram's items of power.

It was small comfort, really.

They gazed at each other silently, leaning on opposite walls. Ram had put on a good face before, keeping up spirits with his trademark good humor. That was gone now, replaced by sad eyes and a serious set to his mouth. For him, this was not just a good-bye to Sky, but to the human city he'd guarded for so long.

Traveling between the two worlds via the closes and alleys required special dispensation by Wynd law. It required the traveler to have a bloody good reason, like Old White's Protector status, soon to be gone. Sky understood the law, because it wasn't so terribly long ago that the Wynd was a place of feudal savagery and blatant enslavement of humans. Every Wyndside Lord and Lady had captured human children at one point or another for his or her own amusement. The current powers in the Wynd had seen the damage and put an end to such behavior, but because of this, Wynd Law meant Ram leaving forever.

And yet — "Wait a minute. Are you telling me that a retired Protector doesn't still have special dispensation?" She was fairly sure that was exactly the case, and the way Ram ducked his head confirmed her suspicions.

"It's the principle of the thing, Sky Blue. I upheld Wynd Law for three hundred years. I'd do best to follow it. But speaking of special dispensation," he said quickly, "I was able to get you official Observer status. You will be free to move in the Sideways at will, provided you don't abuse the privilege. Since I won't be here to give you express permission anymore."

"How did you manage that?" She was delighted, but shocked.

"I argued that you had the right to choose the world of humans as your side rather than the Wynd, being a half-human, but should still be able to enjoy your Wyndling heritage. I vouched for your lack of interest in human domination, too. That, and frankly you aren't powerful enough to concern them."

That last bit made the most sense. More importantly, it meant that she could still visit Ram…albeit maybe once a year, at most. She couldn't be seen to be abusing her privileges.

Ram touched her shoulder, making sure she looked at his face. "I also sincerely want you to keep watch, Summer Sky Blue. That's why I gave you my tools. I don't know who my successor will be, but I trust you to care for Edinburgh as I would. Keep watch for us both, and report to the Protector if you see anything wrong."

She found herself nodding solemnly, although part of her still didn't understand why he was asking this. Perhaps it was just that she was a known quantity, for all her own powers were limited.

But of course she would do what she could. For Ram. For Old White. For the closest thing to a father she'd ever had.

She let out a long breath. "I guess this is where I leave you, then." It wasn't as though he was dying. He just wasn't going to be here. He was the only person in her life around whom she could be her true self, and she would only see him rarely, now. Very rarely.

Ram enfolded her in his arms, and she found she had nothing more to say. "Take care, my Sky Blue," he said quietly. "Keep your eyes and heart open. I would have stayed…" he trailed off and she blinked, startled. But then he released her abruptly and swiped at his eyes.

"Off you go then."

She nodded as he stepped back. Placing her hand on the wall of the Close, Sky let the power that lay in the bones of its stonework, the power fueled by the spirit of the city, by the vibrant lives of millions who had worked and loved and lived inside its walls, pull her back to the world and to Edinburgh.

⊷

His words still bothered her, days later. Why had he seemed reluctant to leave after all? Why was he so insistent that she should keep watch?

Certainly, she had been a casual informant through the years they had known each other, but she had never thought of it as a job description. She had a perfectly adequate human job at the Bank of Scotland. It wasn't as though Ram or any other Wyndling had paid her to watch the streets of Edinburgh.

But to be fair, she always had done that to a certain degree. Edinburgh was the kind of city that required your attention. Once her hooks were in you, your heart would be completely hers forever.

Sky had spoken to countless people at the bank, people who had once been tourists and had fallen in love with the city.

Some fell for the classical, ordered beauty of the New Town, where graceful Georgian townhouses held court in clean lines, their walls the color of honey and smoke.

Some, like Sky, had given their heart to the Old town, with its jumbled mix of buildings ranging from the medieval to the postmodern, its throngs of tourists — all noise and color — heading for the castle. And of course its myriad alleyways in the forms of old closes, courts, and wynds, all trailing off of the main spine of the Royal Mile, each quaintly still bearing its name from the past, even when a modern building engulfed it. Each bearing the weight of history and memory in its bones, a power that uniquely tied it to the Sidewynd.

Being who she was, how could Sky ever have resisted this place?

So she watched now, from the closes and the courts. Ram's replacement still hadn't arrived yet — or if he/she/it had, they hadn't seen fit to seek Sky out. So she wandered to the Old Town every moment she wasn't working at the bank. Even on her breaks she found herself looking through the Eye that Ram had left her, a small disc of milky glass that would, if she concentrated on it long enough, reveal parts of the city to her -- especially parts like the Royal Mile, where the power was strong and the connection to the Wynd was at its closest.

She wore Ram's amulets now, although she still hadn't found the papers that described what each was supposed to do. It was a way of keeping him close, and that was what mattered right now. She had the Universal Map tucked in her purse, but knew the city well enough that she hadn't opened it yet. Whenever she finished work, she would check the Eye and make her way to whatever place showed on its surface. Nothing seemed to happen under her observation, but she didn't mind watching the city every day. She never minded.

Then, one week after she and Ram had parted ways, something happened.

It was early evening. Sky had leaned against the gate of a private close, in the section of the Royal Mile known as High Street, to eat her take-away curry and watch a young couple in their late teens — definitely tourists — take a meandering tour down the length of the Royal Mile, from Castlehill to Canongate.

At least, she assumed that was their goal, as they seemed to be stopping in every close, court, and wynd that was open enough for them to duck inside, or at least peer past the gates.

Oblivious to the intermittent summer rain, they had already come up the South side of High Street, crossed over, and headed down the North side. Sky very much enjoyed their delight in reading aloud the names — Toddrick's Wynd, World's End Close, Fleshmarket Close — and trying to figure out where the alleys led.

The Eye had indicated this place, and something about that young couple pulled Sky's attention. She could focus her observation skills very well, if she so chose — including hearing words spoken across the busy street, in the rain, with many conversations swirling between. The couple was American, she thought. Or possibly Canadian. The boy — lanky, blond, with a crooked nose and a rock band T-shirt, was explaining to the girl — petite, with Asian features, similarly dressed — that they could totally move to Scotland if one of them went to college here. Or got a job at the museum. Or something.

Ah, youthful optimism.

Then, she felt a tug at her insides, one that indicated Sideway activity of some kind. It came from across the street. Bailie Fyfe's Close. Right as the young duo had ducked in by the gate to escape a particularly vigorous downpour from the capricious Scottish weather.

Coincidence? Not bloody likely.

Cursing under her breath, Sky dodged across the road, trusting her not-quite-human speed and luck to get her there in one piece. The magic flared as her feet landed on the curb of the North side, and faded as she ducked around an elderly couple heading into a kilt shop.

When she got to Bailie Fyfe's Close, the youngsters were nowhere to be seen.

Of course they weren't.

Due to the sudden downpour, the sidewalk had fewer people than usual and most of them had had their heads down. None looked shocked to see a pair of kids suddenly vanish, although a skilled user of the Sideways would be able to hide signs of passing at any rate. One oncoming young man looked mildly bemused at Sky's hasty arrival and frantic search around the close and the restaurant next door, but he moved on.

Something in her gut told her the couple had been pulled through a Sideway. She doubted it was by choice.

It seemed she was the only one who could do anything about it, so she ducked around the corner and pulled a "forget me" glamour over herself — a particularly difficult trick, but she had practiced it under Ram's tutelage until she could do it at a moment's notice, provided she had the power for it. Then she put her hand on the stones and pulled herself into the Wynd.

It was only after she stepped out into the Spine that it occurred to her that this wasn't her job. She was supposed to be observing, not Protecting.

Well, she was all those two had, and she was here now.

No sign of them on the street in front of her. Something tugged between her shoulder-blades and made her turn around and look through the close she had just exited. Intuition, maybe, or perhaps one of Ram's little tools…

Or just common sense, because where the closes of Edinburgh led to other parts of the city, their equivalents Wyndside led to other parts of the Wynd itself.

In this case, Bailie Fyfe's Close led from the Spine to what appeared to be a copse of trees, with hills beyond. And there, three tall Wyndlings escorted two smaller, familiar figures through the trees.

This was not good.

Sky's sharpened sight marked out a tall, willowy sort in the front, with long, pale-gold hair. The other two were clearly some sort of muscle, chosen to intimidate. One seemed to be made of rocks. The other was of a similar type to Old White, although distinctly more goatlike, with short horns and brown-and-black coloring.

The two youngsters clung to each other. She couldn't see their faces, but she could imagine the dazed confusion of emotions they must be feeling right now. And she was going to be the one to get them back?

Surely this wasn't even within her meager capabilities, let alone her job description.

But Old White was off making a home in some peaceful corner of the Wynd. The new Protector had never arrived. Clearly these Wyndlings thought they could get away with the older, darker ways — snatching human children away for their own amusement — because no one currently guarded the Sideways, upholding the reformed Wynd laws.

Well, Sky knew enough Wynd law to keep herself from inadvertently breaking any rules; Ram had made sure of that. And she also knew that what those three Wyndlings were doing was quite illegal.

And it appeared that she was the only one in any position to stop it.

So she followed after the group, frantically going over her available actions. She couldn't take any of them on in a fight of physical skill or magic, but they didn't necessarily know that. They might recognize that she was only a half-Wyndling, but she also had Old White's tools of authority.

Now there was a thought. Sky untucked Ram's amulets from inside her shirt as she approached, hoping they might help.

Her only choice was to brazen this out.

They had noticed her now. The two Wyndling muscle turned to confront her, and she schooled the trepidation from her face. She drew on a bit of her limited power to amplify and project her voice, to give it badly-needed authority.

"You are breaking Wynd law. Release the humans immediately."

The leader — the one with the long hair — had turned as well. He was one of those 'unearthly beauty' types, with cheekbones sharp enough to cut, and eyes the same pale gold as his hair. He wore traditional robe-like garments, also pale yellow, rather than the modern human dress that many Wyndlings had adopted these days.

He looked her up and down, his gaze sharpening on the amulets she wore. "Impossible. There is no Protector in Old Town."

The goat-man turned to his leader, his voice a low rumble. "Alabaster, you said our Lord had arranged — "

Alabaster silenced him with a hiss. Sky swiftly buried her shock.

Instead, she barked a laugh. "Your Lord was mistaken, clearly." Inwardly she thought furiously. Was one of the Lords pulling strings with the powers that be? Had Ram's retirement not been entirely voluntary? Was there truly no other protector coming?

The eyes of the two teenagers were fastened on her face, huge and desperate. She had to keep talking. She had to be convincing. Especially with the rock creature and the goat-man beginning to look uncertain, glancing between her and Alabaster.

She planted her feet and faced Alabaster squarely, resisting the urge to clutch at Ram's amulets or take any action that appeared uncertain about her authority. "Release the human children to me, and your actions will have only been an infraction. If you attempt to take them further, I will stop you, and the law will come down upon you." It had better.

Alabaster pursed his lips and looked her over more carefully. "No, I don't think so, halfblood girl. They would never appoint someone like you to protect the Sideways. Be gone." He flicked a hand at her, and she felt a force attempting to pick her up and fling her back toward the close from which they'd come.

One of the amulets on her chest flared with warmth. Somehow, her feet stayed where they were.

Bless Ram.

Still, even with protection she could be no match for the three Wyndlings.

But the close, now — if she could bring them back there somehow, she would be on home ground. She could catch the attention of some denizens of the Spine, perhaps. Get enough people involved, and Alabaster would have to give up. Wouldn't he?

The pale man was quickly recovering from the surprise of his failed spell. Although Sky's heart quailed, she strode forward, glaring at the goat-man and the rock creature, daring them to make a move. They didn't. Yet.

She grabbed the boy and the girl by their arms. "Run for the doorway. Now," she hissed, and shoved them behind her. She clutched at the pendants around her neck and thought of that feeling of resistance. Could she amplify it long enough to keep Alabaster and his lackeys from moving forward? Long enough to get the children back to Bailie Fyfe's Close?

The three Wyndlings leaped forward, and she pushed back with everything she had.

It worked.

The Wyndlings strained against the invisible force, enraged. She gritted her teeth and felt herself slipping. She had little magic of her own — this was all the amulet, and it wouldn't hold for long.

She glanced behind her and saw that the two humans had reached the mouth of the close. They halted inside, unsure of how to proceed.

She slipped another inch. Could she get to them in time, if she let the spell go? Now would be an excellent time to have some force flinging her toward the door again. Could she...? She tried to remember how that had felt. Clutching the pendant, she envisioned its force of resistance as a quick blast outward instead.

The spell ended with a bang and she flew backwards, landing winded in front of the stone opening. Perfect, although painful.

No time to congratulate herself. The force had been much less effective against the strength of Alabaster and his muscle, and they leaped toward her now.

She scrambled into the narrow alleyway, urging the humans toward the other door. The power of the stones, of Edinburgh and humans and memory, remained the same — Wyndside or not.

This was home. This was hers.

"ENOUGH!" she bellowed as Alabaster reached the doorway. "I

will not let you break Wynd law. Have you no respect for the powers that be?" Appealing loudly to the law should draw other Wyndling attention, she hoped.

"You are not the law, halfblood girl. Give me what is mine." His voice was cold, but she noticed he spoke quietly.

So of course she spoke louder. "Nothing of the human world is yours, Alabaster. Who do you think you are, flouting the law and taking human children?" Oh, that had gotten some attention. A small crowd began to gather on the Spine side, peering through the close doorway to see who the lawbreaker might be.

She stared him down, daring him to argue further. Yes, I will shout your name some more. Yes, I will cause as big a stink as I can. Your Lord might be pulling strings somewhere, but I doubt even he can openly flout Wynd law.

Alabaster's gaze was a cold knife. "This isn't over, false Protector," he said softly, and she shivered involuntarily. But he motioned his lackeys away and faded out of sight.

She couldn't waste time thinking about what she had just done. "Stay close," she said to her charges, and put her hand on the stone of Bailie Fyfe's Close.

A pulling sensation, and they were through. "Quickly now," she hissed, pushing at the bewildered humans to get them through to the sidewalk, hastily remembering to pull her glamour back on. She had a feeling this wasn't quite over yet.

The children stood outside the kilt shop now, blinking at Sky through a light drizzle of rain. They hadn't said a word Wyndside, which made her wonder if Alabaster had bespelled them somehow. Now, the boy burst out, "You had a tail!"

She gaped at him. Really? "And you were just kidnapped by fairies," she said flatly. "You might say thank you," she prompted as they stared.

The girl spoke for the first time. "Thank you," she said. She shivered.

"Why did this happen to us?"

Not the worst question she could ask. But Sky wasn't sure how to answer. "I don't know why you, specifically. But I think something is changing here. Someone from the other side wants humans, and I'm going to find out why." More than ever, she wanted Ram back. Especially since his absence was clearly the impetus for this blatant break in Wynd law.

The boy and girl continued to stare at her, and she sighed. She had been taught a spell of forgetting when Ram decided she might need to protect her identity, but she didn't want to use it. She wanted these two to stay alert. "Don't go into any more closes," she said. "Or courts, or wynds. Are you going home soon?"

"Tomorrow," the girl managed.

"Good. I wish—"

Power built up nearby. Paisley Close. It had to be Alabaster. Who knew what he would try to do?

Sky couldn't get there in time.

But maybe she didn't need to. The power of Edinburgh hummed in the concrete under her feet, in the old stones and the new plexiglass and everything in between. It was more faint than what lay in the closes, but it was hers.

She might be half Wyndling and half East Indian, but she was all Scottish, thank you very much.

She focused on Paisley Close and pushed.

The force on the other side sharpened. She could picture Alabaster growing angrier with every passing second.

But she held on, because this was her city.

Edinburgh had always had Sky's heart. Now Edinburgh had her protection, too. And in return, the city was Sky's power.

The pushing stopped and the power drained away.

Sky stayed alert, knowing she must appear rather odd, standing on the sidewalk facing toward Paisley Close, her eyes closed and fists clenched. The kids still stood behind her, questions in their eyes.

"He's trying to come back. You should go back to your hotel," she said. "I think you will be safest there." They nodded mutely and all but ran down the street.

She kept them in her sights until they reached the road that would take them to New Town, but stayed on the Royal Mile as the sky darkened. If Alabaster — or anyone else — tried to use another Sideway before night fell, Sky would stop him.

She'd have to get a new apartment in Old Town, she realized. She might have to quit her job, although she had no idea how she would manage.

No other protector was coming. Maybe Ram had known this all along. Maybe he had left her his tools because he knew she would take on his mantle. He knew her better than anyone, after all.

Sly old goat.

Against all common sense, Sky found herself smiling. She had a feeling she would need to dig up those papers when she got home. And then she'd get about the business of protecting her city.

☞ E<small>ND</small> ☜

THE FLAT ABOVE THE WYND

This story represents a bit of an addiction. Specifically, the city of Edinburgh. On all of my trips to Scotland (three — and counting!) I continued to be fascinated by The Royal Mile. So much so that on my last trip, I spent several full days wandering Old Town for 'research.'

That was when I realized all the marvelous little details and settings I found could not be contained in just one story. So of course I had to write a sequel to "Sidewynd," in what would become a short fiction series I call the Wyndside Stories.

And now, due to the urging of several fellow writers and editors, Sky's Wyndside adventures are on their way to becoming a novel!

Sky glared at the (entirely too long) spiral of chipped red stairs and cursed Ram once more.

Not aloud, mind you, and not with any real intent. Being only half Wyndling meant she wasn't terribly strong in magic, but she'd rather not risk her theoretical cursing becoming a real fairy curse through sheer carelessness. Especially not when her beloved former mentor was enjoying a well-deserved retirement in the Wynd.

She hoped.

But right now, she desperately wished him here by Lady Stairs. Because she wanted his counsel, especially now as she was trying to pick up where he left off. Because she missed Ramsay "Old White" Whitebridge more than her own long-absent father.

And, most importantly, because she *really* wanted to give Ram a piece of her mind.

He could have had a flat anywhere in Edinburgh's Old Town, as long as there was an active human close or wynd nearby. By the end of his 300-year tenure as Protector of all the Sideways along the Royal Mile, he had a *very* comfortable living from his long-term investments.

Sky knew this, because it was all hers now.

So, when he could have had any flat he chose, why had he chosen Lady Stairs Close?

Her ire wasn't about the long flight of stairs, not really. Any location along the Royal Mile would have that problem, since there would always be shops below. (Although he could have chosen something other than the very, very top.)

It was just that this spot was so…central.

So full of people. All the time.

People always trying to climb *these* bloody stairs. Because someone had helpfully labeled them and now the damn tourists thought they were part of the Lady Stairs Close experience. Lovely green James Court, even more picturesque honey-and-smoke-colored Makar's Court, the Writers' Museum…and the red stairs that *clearly* must be the famed Lady Stairs the close was named for.

(They were not.)

Sky liked people. She liked the noise and color and bustle of Old Town, from the nigh-constant drone of the bagpipes to the crack of the street performer's whips to the sidewalks cluttered with displays of tartans and kilts from the dozen wool-and-cashmere shops that populated her block alone. Unlike many of her former (human) coworkers from the banking job, she even liked these late-summer crowds of tourists.

But she didn't like them climbing the stairs to her flat. Every day. All day.

So why here, Ram? Sky would never in a million years try to use Lady Stairs to cross over into the Wynd — it was far too popular, although its popularity certainly gave it more power than some of the other Sideways. And now she would have to be extra careful about her appearance *in her own home*, with the risk of random folk coming up the stairs…and possibly seeing a silhouette that didn't look…human.

Not to mention the inconvenience right at this very moment, waiting for the most recent tourist — English, she thought — to realize he was blocking the way to her flat. Walloper. No clue he was keeping her from her job, of course.

Which was *not* to be standing at the foot of the stairs and wishing she was elsewhere.

Her job was to go upstairs, look into the Eye, read a few more pages of the stacks and stacks of notes Ram left her…and then don her amulets and be ready to start her patrol by late afternoon.

Before the dusk and the twilight.

When doors might open.

When anything could happen.

She tried to block out the chatter and steps on the stairs — here came another group, kids this time, just lovely, thanks — and concentrate on what she was reading.

Wynd Law was infinitely more twisty and tricky than she'd ever imagined. And she had learned quite a lot of it, growing up with one foot in Edinburgh and one in the Wynd; with her status as a half-Wyndling, she'd known to be careful. But as Protector — albeit an unofficial one — her responsibilities now tripled. And, if she wanted to keep doing Ram's work without fear of interference from the Wynd, the laws that bound her tripled too.

Laws she had already broken, less than a month ago.

She hadn't known better. She hadn't even known she would be assuming Ram's mantle at the time. So she had let two teenagers, two Lost Children, go back home with their memories intact…and now she had no idea how that would affect her future.

If other Wyndlings ever found out, that is.

A faint glow pulsed from the Far-Seeing Eye, and Sky welcomed the chance to stop rubbing her temples and look at her first location for patrol.

The documents Ram had left her about the Eye vaguely said it was 'tuned to receive echoes of possible futures,' which sounded like it *ought* to mean something. What it meant in practical terms was the Eye sent her an image of somewhere in Old Town…and most often, nothing would happen when she got there.

On the days something *did* happen, however…

Luckily there had been no repeats of that first, fateful incident.

Yet.

She picked up the circle of normally-milky glass and peered into it. The misty depths had cleared, revealing…the foot of her own stairs?

She frowned and shook it. Had her own internal complaints affected it, somehow?

Impossible. There were too many safeguards on this, the most necessary of her Protector's tools. The Eye was even keyed to this very flat, so it would vanish and return here should it ever be forcefully removed from Sky's possession. She could only imagine the kind of power that would go into a spell like that. Her own meagre abilities couldn't compare.

The disc pulsed with pale light again, revealing the same image. No question about it, they were the red-painted steps she had glared at less than an hour ago.

The pulses of light came faster, somehow insistent. The Eye had never done that before.

Fine and well and good. Grimacing, Sky stood and drew on her faded green summer-weight anorak, stuffing the disc of glass into a hidden inner pocket and tucking Ram's jumble of amulets down her shirt. She checked her glamour in the mirror — yes, still the ordinary brown skin and brown eyes of a mid-thirty-ish East Indian woman; no odd blue eyes or furred, plume-like tail to be seen — and grumbled to herself as she exited the flat and headed for the stairs.

Because of the twisty nature of the stairwell, Sky almost ran into the girl standing at the base, frowning down at a slip of paper in her hand. A slight, dark-haired teenager with a pretty face, possibly Japanese heritage. Ripped jeans and a black t-shirt with some rock band or another, heavy satchel over one shoulder.

Sky knew her instantly.

The girl looked up and her eyes widened. "You!"

Sky tried to school her shock into something calmer. She had never thought she'd see this child again.

Not after what they'd been through, merely three weeks before.

"What are you doing here?" Sky asked, her mind racing. At the back of her head, a thought began to flash, a reminder of the Wynd law she had just read. The rules she had broken with this very human girl. And now, a sudden, serendipitous opportunity to fix things.

With Wynd magic, serendipity should *always* be highly suspect.

So.

She needed more information.

The girl was still frozen, surprise written all over her face. "I—" She shook her head, as if trying to clear it. "I — hang on. What are you doing here?" More likely American tourist than Canadian, Sky thought, revising her first impression from last month.

Sky ignored the girl's clumsy deflection. "I thought you were going home. You said you left the next day." She remembered the conversation very clearly. The girl and her (Sky assumed) blond boyfriend had been shaken from the near-kidnapping they had just experienced — but of the two of them, the girl had seemed the more quick-witted at the time.

"Kevin left. I stayed." The girl chewed her lip, looking down at her hands, which clenched and unclenched. Sky wondered if the short response hid still-fresh pain over a breakup.

"Why?" Sky asked, more gently. "Why would you stay? You know it's not safe."

"Oh no, I was careful! I didn't come back to the Royal Mile," the girl protested. "I mean—" she turned red as Sky arched an eyebrow and looked around pointedly. "Not until now. I had to get answers. I had to know what happened. And I couldn't find you again, and…" she trailed off, and looked at her hands again.

Sky kept her bearing, but inside her emotions churned. What a right bourach this was, as Ram would say. A mess she had made because she hadn't known what she was doing in the slightest.

She'd need to do better, this time.

Much better.

The girl looked up, chewing her lip once more. She glanced around at the people milling about Makar's Court beyond the stairwell, then back at Sky. "I guess…can we talk somewhere more private?" she asked. She peered upstairs, past Sky's shoulder.

Privacy was a very good idea, but the girl was not getting invited to Sky's flat.

Unless you just erased her memories afterward, a small part of her mind whispered. Sky pushed the thought aside, not liking the queasy feeling it produced.

She didn't *want* this kind of responsibility.

"Follow me," Sky said, moving past the girl and into the late afternoon sunlight. Her patrol would normally begin soon. But the Eye had clearly wanted her here, and for good reason.

Still, best to be sure. She surreptitiously tugged the disc from her pocket, noting that it had turned milky again. Good enough.

"By the way," Sky said, pausing before they entered the sidewalks, "What's your name? You can call me Sky."

The girl turned red again. "Oh shit — I mean, uh. I hadn't even thought of that." She stuck out a hand. "I'm Morgan."

Sky took Morgan's hand and smiled encouragingly. "I didn't think of it myself. We *were* a bit busy. Now follow me; I've got just the spot for a chat — if you don't mind about seven minutes of walking."

Trunk's Close was both old and quiet, making it one of the better Sideways. But when it wasn't being used for that purpose, it was also the way into a little public garden: one of her favorite places in the world, and seldom populated by tourists.

Today was no exception. Sky would never grow tired of the way the clamor of the streets seemed to vanish when one stepped into the closes and courts that led off from the spine that was The Royal Mile. No magic needed; the old stones and structures of the city itself did the work.

But she felt power humming through her bones all the same. The quiet, slow power that lay in Edinburgh, grown from the weight of history, the humans who lived and died and believed in things unseen, back and back to the medieval roots of the city. The power that Wyndlings like Sky and Ram could draw on, when they stepped into the Wynd and back again.

And for Sky, the power was love. Love for this place, love for the humans in it.

And *that* was what had called her to take on Ram's mantle, despite her fears.

It was good to remember that.

She stepped into the garden, Morgan walking quietly behind her. The sound of the streets faded into the relative hush of the green space, the rustle of the great oak tree that graced most of the garden.

Morgan peered around her with wide eyes. "I didn't even know this was here," she said, her voice soft. Sky wondered if she could feel it too. The weight, the stillness. *Could* humans feel the old power of Edinburgh, and simply not have a name for it?

Sky had no one to ask but Morgan…and now was not the time.

"Now," she said, gesturing to the bench, "Let's start. How did you find me?"

Morgan frowned. "Wait, I thought I got to ask *you* questions."

Teenagers.

"Let's make it a two-way conversation," Sky said, managing to suppress an eye-roll. "I need to know what brought you to Lady Stairs. Especially when you knew you should be avoiding Old Town."

"It was the group I found online. You know, the support group."

The *what?*

"I'm sorry, what support group?"

"The group for other people like me. People who," the girl gulped, and lowered her voice to a whisper. "Uh. *Who've crossed over into the fairy realm.*" She muttered something else under her breath that Sky couldn't quite catch.

But Sky's mind was reeling already.

Shit.

Bollocks.

And some other words of which Sky's dear mother would strongly disapprove.

What was Sky supposed to do? No one had warned her about this. She'd no idea such a thing existed.

You know what you have to do, that voice in the back of her head whispered. *Damage control.*

You have to find the whole group and erase all *of those dangerous memories.*

Morgan peered at her face, frowning. "Um, Sky? Are you all right?"

She had not thought to school her expression into something properly neutral.

And there was no way to bluff her way out of this, especially with this burning need to know *exactly* what the teenager was talking about. Sky was going to have to use at least partial honesty, now. "I actually was unaware of the existence of a support group," she said, and her concerned frown did not need to be faked. "If they had my address, they should have contacted me." She started to build an argument for why Morgan should get the group together and take her to them immediately, but was arrested by the girl's next words.

"Oh, so that *was* your address? It was supposed to be this old white-haired guy. That's what the others said."

For the second — no, third — time today, Sky felt like she'd been hit with a sledgehammer.

Ram had known about this?

Morgan was still talking. "…but when I saw you, it kind of went out my head because I knew you and, you know, you were the one I wanted to talk to all along anyway. Do you know an old white-haired guy?"

Dammit, Ram. I need you back here.

More than ever.

"I do," Sky said, quickly getting her thoughts untangled. "He protected Old Town before me. He did what I do now."

Morgan's voice was hushed. "You — you save people who were… kidnapped by fairies. So he did that too. That makes sense."

Sky nodded. Watching over Old Town was her true purpose. And she needed to protect it at all costs; she couldn't forget that.

"Is he…dead?" the girl asked.

"Just retired," Sky assured her. Retired and well beyond her grasp. Deep in the Wynd now, bound by the very laws he had enforced, never to return to the human city again. She might see him again in a year or so, if she was lucky. It stung still.

Especially now that she suspected it had been a forced retirement. For a purpose she hadn't yet uncovered.

And now there was this.

A new mystery on her hands.

"I guess I should tell them," Morgan said slowly. "They have old information." She brightened, no doubt pleased to be of some use.

Time to seize the opportunity while she could. "I could speak to them too," Sky said. "If Ram — that's the old man — was a friend of theirs, then I should be a part of this."

The list of questions was growing by the second, but at least she had her next move sorted.

❧

The prospect of introducing the support group to Sky had apparently driven the rest of the girl's questions out of her head, which was extremely convenient. They found a cafe with free wi-fi so Morgan could get out her laptop and contact the other members.

The drinks had just arrived — tea for Sky, of course, and coffee for the American — when she felt a warm pulse in her inner coat pocket, and grimaced. She had nearly forgotten the rest of her job.

The Eye showed her an area near St. Giles' Cathedral. "I have to go keep watch again," she told Morgan, reluctantly. "Do you have a phone you can use here?"

The American shook her head. "Just my brother's, and he's still working at the University, I think. He's usually there until seven."

Sky filed that information away for later. "Why don't you arrange a meeting with your group and then contact me later, when you can borrow his phone," she said.

She needed time to think, anyway.

She had far, far too much to try to understand.

❧

As dusk started to fall — fairly late, of course, because it was a summer evening — Sky paced near St. Giles' Cathedral, thinking furiously.

Ram had clearly been involved with this so-called "support group," and had not said a word to her about it. He clearly hadn't followed Wynd law, either. Why?

Much as she loved the sly old goat, Old White was as tricky as any other Wyndling out there. He most likely had some canny plan she couldn't possibly understand with her slightly-too-human brain.

Damn him. This put her in a terrible bind.

Her phone rang — at the same moment that the Eye pulsed against her chest.

She juggled the two inexpertly, nearly attempting to put the glass disc to her ear. Finally she managed to sort them out and answer the unfamiliar number before the ringing stopped. "It's me," said Morgan's breathless voice on the other end. "This is really weird."

"What's weird?" Sky said, squinting at the Eye's image. It still showed the very area where she stood. She felt no change to the magic all around her. No increases of power at any of the closes or wynds nearby.

How very concerning, especially taken with its behavior earlier today.

"Ravi said I shouldn't trust you, that you were lying. I told him that was bullshit," she said indignantly, but Sky heard it with half an ear, trying to walk a little further down, get a better view of the street side with the higher number of closes. "He said that the old guy, Ramsay something-or-other, hadn't retired because he just spoke to him, like, three days ago!"

Sky stopped short, right there on the crowded walk. Several passersby cursed and stumbled around her.

Impossible.

Under Wynd law, his retirement had been final. He had given over his responsibilities, his flat, his wealth and all of his magical items, over to her.

Hadn't he?

What *was* the old man's game?

"Sky? Are you still there?"

"Yes, yes — I just don't know why he'd be here," Sky said. "I was with him when he signed everything over to me." She didn't know why she was telling the child this. Just thinking out loud. Nothing made sense.

"Ravi said the old man had finally come around," Morgan said. "That — that after years of trying to convince him, he was finally letting the…" her voice faded out, then came back. "First wave? I think? Letting us — them, I mean — cross back over again." Her voice dropped to a nearly inaudible whisper with the last words.

The phone slipped out of Sky's nerveless fingers and clattered to the ground.

This was insanity.

No humans ever crossed back over a second time.

Every Wyndling knew it was too dangerous, for the Wynd and for the humans themselves.

It had never occurred to her that a human would want to. Especially the Lost Children, the ones taken against their will.

But…she realized now, suddenly: Morgan had said that very thing, in the garden.

Sky had barely heard it, barely noticed while her brain had been churning with everything else. *"Who've crossed over into the fairy realm…and want to go back."*

Oh, this was much, much worse than she had thought.

Sky picked up the phone with trembling fingers. The screen was cracked, but it still looked functional. The call was still going. "Sky? Sky? What happened?"

The Eye flared again.

"Did he say *where* they were going?" If it was happening right now, or soon, maybe that was what the Eye was trying to tell her.

"No, but I followed them. I think we're going to one of the…closes by the cathedral?"

Sky couldn't draw breath to speak. Her gaze was pulled up the street, to Byre's Close, where a stooped old man in a kilt, with wild, white hair, was unlocking the private gate and gesturing to a young East Indian man standing behind him, carrying some kind of case.

And — yes. Skye's eyes were Wyndling-sharp. There was the slim figure in the black t-shirt, trailing them half a block back.

"Morgan, I need you to go back, out of Old Town, and stay with your brother," she choked out, already dodging pedestrians and wayward vehicles on her way across the street. "I've got to talk to Ram before—" before what? He did something foolish, dangerous, possibly evil?

"But I could—"

She tried to stay calm. "This is between me and Ram, understand? Let me handle it. I'll call this number back later. All right?"

"Okay, but—" Morgan said, and Sky threw her phone into her pocket without another word.

The magic flared inside Byre's Close. Sky reached the locked gate and looked around quickly. No sign of Morgan, but she hadn't been close enough to get pulled through. Sky couldn't waste any more minutes looking around for the girl.

She used a bit of not-very-finessed power to get the gate unlocked again. It cost her precious moments, and the magic from the Sideway was already fading again by the time she got inside.

She hadn't even thrown on her 'forget me,' so curious heads were turning to watch her rush. She stumbled in a little further, pulling the glamour over herself. Out of sight, out of mind.

Then she stilled herself long enough to feel the power in the bones of the city. Joy and pain and memory, creativity and belief and the weight of history. This was what drew Wyndlings to the old, old closes and wynds and courts; this was what kept the Sideways open, year after year. A connection no one could explain.

She closed her eyes and let the magic pull her across into the Wynd.

Stepping into the Spine, the Wyndside equivalent to the Royal Mile, was always a disorienting experience. Colors were too bright, even in the pale green light of fairy dusk, and seemed to carry tangible weight, even taste. The buildings echoed those on the human side, but only just. They were the wrong sizes or materials, or sometimes simply impossible by the laws of physics.

Pipes wailed on this street-side, too, but their sound was wilder even than human bagpipes. Sweet and wild and eerie, and their player was a silvery creature with a few too many arms and gossamer cobweb wings. Whirring filled the air and Sky ducked a flight of tiny winged beings, what the humans would likely call pixies.

The air tasted like honey and felt like the brush of silk against her skin.

As she always did, Sky recalled vividly the first time she had crossed over. As a clueless teenager herself, only just discovering her incomprehensible paternal heritage.

In all the years following, these first few seconds Wyndside never lost their potency. Like a strong whiskey…for *all* the senses.

Sky forced herself to reorient, to focus. She had to find Ram, but he was nowhere to be seen. He'd be Old White here, in his true form, a towering half-man with goat-gargoyle feet and horns curling in his wild white mane of hair.

She didn't see any of that.

"Oh, *wow.*"

Oh, no. Skye whirled around, her stomach dropping.

Of course. Morgan. She must have followed Sky in while her eyes were closed. How could she have been so stupid? Both of them. *Stupid.*

Morgan's eyes were huge as she spun in a slow circle. "I had forgotten," she whispered. "I had forgotten how *magical* it was. Everything's so… God. I don't even know. So real. And unreal. At the same time. Like a drug."

"You can't be here!" Sky shouted. Morgan flinched and jerked back toward her.

"You don't—"

"It's dangerous, Morgan," Sky said, interrupting whatever stupid teenager thing was about to come out of the girl's mouth. "You shouldn't even need me to tell you that."

Morgan stared at her. "You're so beautiful. I forgot that too."

Sky's own changes were much more subtle than a full Wyndling. Her true self was Summer Sky Blue: golden-furred ears and silken tail added to her usual human appearance, eyes changed to a color so blue as to be unnatural.

It was normally a relief to drop her glamour here, but not today.

"We don't have time for this," she snapped. She grabbed Morgan's hand. Whatever else happened here, she couldn't risk letting the child out of her sight.

She drew her breath to shout for Ram, but something stopped her. Raised voices, up the street, toward the crystal-hued Wynd equivalent of Edinburgh Castle.

"Where is Ram Whitebridge?" a very human male voice shouted. "What kind of trick is this?"

Sky started to run toward the voice, dragging Morgan with her. She didn't dare tell the human girl to stay here in the Spine. It would be just as dangerous as not, and then Sky wouldn't be around if something happened.

There were no good solutions to this.

"I think someone is snatching your friends," she said grimly to the girl, whose eyes were still huge, her head craning from side to side as they ran. "Using trickery."

As opposed to the sheer balls that Fae Lord Alabaster had used last month, simply opening a Sideway and pulling Morgan and her boyfriend through as they ducked inside Bailie Fyfe's Close to escape a downpour.

Did that mean this was more of the same, but the criminal element had simply gotten sneakier when they realized Skye would oppose them?

Either way, it didn't bode well.

The shouts cut off abruptly, but Sky could follow where they had been. She rounded down a side street, Morgan in tow.

The alley led to a Wyndside court. Here, that meant a seat of power. Bad. Very, very bad.

The young man who had been with not-Ram was there, gripping his case and gesturing wildly. His face was shouting, but no sound emerged. The other figure with him was like no one Sky had ever seen.

Like many of the lords of the Wynd, the figure wore flowing robes instead of the modern human fashions adopted by many other denizens of the Wynd. These robes were red. Vivid red, deep red, blood and carmine all together. The being inside them was snow-white, paler even than Alabaster had been. On its strangely-elongated head was an intricate tangle of white branches. Its hair? Or merely a headdress?

The Wyndling looked up as Sky approached. She filled her lungs to shout at it, to use the trick she had used before. Draw attention, get Wynd law to come into the picture. Pretend she had all the authority of the Protector behind her.

She never had the chance.

"Be still," the white being hissed.

Its eyes flared bright gold and blue and red, a kaleidoscope of colors. They trapped her, and the shout died in her throat.

Beside her, Morgan went still as well.

The Wyndling cocked its head at the three of them. "This will be fun," it said softly, and made a gesture with its hand.

The world flared white.

⊖

She was trapped in a crystal cage. Shifting colors everywhere gave the impression of a thousand prisms, although when she touched the wall of her cell it was porous to the touch, like lava rock. There were no seams, no windows, nothing but the changing light. And her two dazed companions, clutching each other and staring wildly around them.

Like everything Wyndside, it was beautiful, shifty, and frustrating.

She resisted the urge to scream her frustration. How could she have ever thought she was strong enough, clever enough to take on Old White's mantle with only a quarter of his Wyndling power, if that?

Her amulets and the Eye were gone, of course.

The only power she possessed without them was her affinity for the magic of the Sideways, her love for Edinburgh, and the power that rested within.

She had none of that here.

She looked over at the two humans and tried to keep a calm face, for them. It was all she could do.

"I'm sorry," Morgan whispered. "I didn't know...I thought you were just going to talk to your friend, so I came to...to get Ravi."

You came because you wanted to cross over again, Sky thought. But rebukes would do no good here. This situation was consequence enough.

The other one, the young man, broke out of his reverie. "I—" he stumbled around, searching for words. "I'm Ravi. You must be Sky."

"I am."

"You knew the real Ram?"

"He was my mentor. He's in retirement now. I didn't lie about that, you know." She kept her voice gentle when it really wanted to go sharp.

To distract herself from her annoyance, she looked at Ravi's case. Curiously, it and Morgan's satchel were still with them, whereas all of Sky's items had been stripped of her. They even took her favorite anorak. Bastards.

Her amulets were likely lost forever, but Sky fervently hoped that the Far-Seeing Eye's safeguard spell would work. No telling what the Wyndling Lord might attempt to do with an artifact like that.

No telling how Sky could ever hope to do her job without it.

She couldn't think about that, so she pointed to the case. "What's in that?"

Ravi ducked his head. "My flute," he said. "Ram — I mean, that… person…told me to bring it with me. I thought he was *Ram*, so I did."

Curious, but not useful.

"Anything of use in your satchel, Morgan?" She asked. Of course there wouldn't be, not for their situation, but it gave them something to do.

"Ah — no, not really," the girl said sheepishly. "Just my art supplies, mostly."

Art supplies?

Sky realized how little she knew about this human girl she'd attached to herself. "So you're an artist…" she said, and looked back at Ravi. "And a musician."

"The others are all like that too," Morgan said, eagerly. "I figured that out right away. Everyone in the support group. We paint and sing and compose music, and I think Emma sculpts. Peter writes poetry. Isn't that weird?"

It was.

"Ram helped us," Ravi said. "The real Ram, I mean. Some of us had met him, from before. When we crossed over. For some of us he came and got us."

"Like what you did for Kevin and me," Morgan put in.

"After we started talking to each other, making this group, he helped us…" Ravi searched for words. "Channel our energies, I think he said. To remember the fairyland…I mean, the Wynd, when we made our art and music and writing. To put it all in there. And it did help," he said, misinterpreting Sky's astonished expression, "But I think we… we all wanted to go back. Some part of each of us did, even though it had been beyond scary for most of us."

Morgan nodded, looking ashamed. "I'm sorry. But it's true. I wasn't kidding when I said it was like a drug. It gets into your blood. It's like this wild…dream, or image, in the back of your mind. All the time."

"Or a song," Ravi said.

Sky found herself speechless. She never knew.

And what *had* Ram been up to? If the very memory of the Wynd was like a drug, why had he not spared them of it by taking it away?

"Ram said," Ravi added, breaking into her confused thoughts, "that what we did helped him. And the Wynd. No, that's not quite right. It helped make the doorways stronger, he said. For one day when there would be no danger in traveling them again." His voice dipped into Ram's cadence for a moment.

What did that — what did *any* of this — mean? None of the answers made any more sense than the questions.

She needed to find Ram and ask him everything.

Which meant she — and the humans — needed to get out of here.

Strengthening the Sideways. Why? And *how*?

Regardless, it did them no good now. She would give an entire leg to be near a Wyndside Close right now. A Sideway. That was where her power was. That was where she could be of use.

Then it dropped in on her. One little, silly idea.

Could they *make* a Sideway?

Would it hurt to try?

"Morgan," she said. "Get our your art supplies. Let's see if you've got enough to paint on the wall."

The shifting lights were annoying, but the wall should hold paint. Or charcoal. Hopefully they would be able to see it.

"Ravi. Do you know any classic jigs or reels? How about 'Scotland the Brave?'"

Ravi nodded. "I like that kind of music," he said. "It's why I came to school here in the first place." The look on his face remained mystified.

"We're going to try to make our own Sideway," Sky told them.

Morgan looked up from sorting her pastels and charcoal sticks. "Because our art strengthens the doors," she said. Her eyes were huge. "Do you think it will work?"

"No idea," Sky said honestly. "But it's better than waiting for whatever the bloody snow creature wants from us."

"Bloody snowman," Morgan snickered, and started to smear her charcoal sticks over one wall, creating an outline. Even as rough strokes indicating an archway, the lines took on a beautiful quality under the lights. The colors filled in the 'stones' like stained glass.

Through the archway, Morgan started to sketch buildings. "Try a wool merchant," Sky said. She could picture it in her head, the one near where the piper most often played. Not far from her new flat at Lady Stairs. She started describing it to Morgan, who filled in the colors and shapes like a rough impressionist painting.

"Your turn, Ravi," Sky said. She didn't know if music would draw the Wyndlings, but it was all they had. "Start playing 'Scotland the Brave.'" It was a very tired tune, partly because it was one of the songs the bagpipes always played outside her flat. It also sounded quite odd on the flute, but she did her best to work past that, imagining the piper in her head, playing alongside. She closed her eyes and imagined the wool merchant storefront, the piles of colorful tartans. The bustle of the street and the old, musty stones of the close as she looked out into it.

"Oh my god," Morgan whispered.

Sky didn't open her eyes. But she could *feel* it.

The love. The magic. The connection that drew Wynd and Old Town together.

Morgan took her hand and started walking forward. Sky reached out, imagining stone beneath her fingers. She could hear the pipes now.

Power flared. She heard shouts coming from somewhere. Behind her. She ignored them, drawing on the power of her imagined close…

And pulled them through.

"We did it," Morgan said in awe. Sky opened her eyes. To her right, past Morgan's wide-eyed stare, she could see Lady Stair's close, full of humans and color and noise. To her left stood Ravi, mouth agape.

They'd done it.

Sky smiled, and then frowned.

The angle and tone of the light told her it was mid-morning. Which morning? How long had they been gone? She glanced around quickly as reality crashed back in. Had any humans seen the three of them appear out of nothing?

No one seemed to be staring in shock. Perhaps their luck continued to hold. Perhaps—

"Oh, *shit*," Morgan said, glancing down at her now-dead phone. "Nate is going to *kill* me."

Not good. And worse, the hair on the back of Sky's neck began to prickle. There was a good chance that someone — or some*thing* — would be coming through a nearby close at any moment. Not Lady Stair's; that would be madness, surely.

All the same…

She reached for the hands of Morgan and Ravi on either side of her. She would *not* relinquish them. They needed safety. They needed time to regroup.

Which meant she was going to have to let the humans into her flat, after all.

The sensible Wyndling in the back of Sky's mind gave a tiny sigh of defeat. Fine and well and good.

"Come with me," Sky said grimly.

⬿

To her vast relief, the Eye's safeguards had held.

For there it was, back in her flat, the innocuous glass disc resting on the cheap wood of her table as if she had merely left it there from her preparations of the previous afternoon. (Had it been the previous afternoon?)

The Eye's surface was still. Yet another relief. It told her that all was well, for now.

Without its power, she didn't know what she would have done.

If she could have done anything at all.

Behind her, Morgan swore at her phone again. "It's not the battery. Sky, what should I—"

"Here." Sky shook her head clear, got out her battered laptop, and quickly logged in. Luckily she hadn't brought *that* into the Wynd with her. Her own phone, of course, was as long-gone as her anorak.

She gestured Morgan toward her chair. "Contact your brother. Tell him to come get you at Lady Stairs. Tell him you'll explain the situation when he gets here. Ravi…"

Sky glanced around. The young man was eyeing the great stacks of paper cluttering every surface in the room and whistling under his breath.

She grimaced. This was why she hadn't wanted anyone up here. "Leave that alone," she snapped. At his wounded look, she forced herself to relax. "When Morgan's done I need you to contact every member of your support group. Let them know that Ram is an impostor, and that they mustn't come near the Royal Mile. Just because that creature isn't trying anything right now—" she glanced at the Eye again — "Doesn't mean that it won't again."

Questions tugged at her, but she couldn't address them yet. She had to come up with a plausible explanation for…well, everything.

"Nate's on his way," Morgan announced, hugging herself and looking grim, pale, and determined. Sky didn't blame her. She imagined her own face looked much the same.

Ravi got online and got to work. "They're going to want to come here, you know," he said, over his shoulder. "This is where Ram always said to go if we needed him. Lady Stair's Close."

But it's not safe.

Or was it?

Ram's protections, his powers, they kept this flat and the Eye connected and safeguarded. Perhaps the power reached further.

She had so much more to learn about being a Protector.

But one thing she *did* know.

Oh yes, suddenly, she knew.

Ram had chosen this place, this oh-so-central, recognizable, bustling place, for one reason: so those who needed him could find him.

She straightened her back and drew a deep breath. She still didn't know Ram's game. Really, she knew hardly anything at all.

But she was all the Lost Children had now. And she was bloody well going to be their Protector.

She'd be the Protector anywhere she needed to be in Old Town.

And right here, in Lady Stair's Close.

☙ END ❧

BANOFFEE PIE AND BLACK PUDDING

This was my Mom's very first favorite story of mine, the first time she convinced me I was a professional writer just waiting to happen. It was also the inspiration for this collection.

As I may have hinted at previously, my obsession with all things Celtic started when I was a small child (thanks, Mom!) and has never faded. It only compounded when I was nineteen, and my whole family visited Ireland for the first time…

(Again, thanks, Mom!)

One of the other obsessions we share is gourmet food. During our trips, we make it a habit of sampling the same dessert — in Ireland's case, Banoffee Pie — in every pub and restaurant we find it.

About five years later, this story was born during a writing challenge for contemporary fantasy with Irish mythology. Perfect!

Alyssa Granville scraped together the remainder of her Banoffee Pie and scooped it into her mouth with a sigh of sheer luxury. The toffee was rich and buttery, and brought the banana and chocolate together in a symphony of flavors, and the whipped cream was the perfect finish. One could easily contemplate the meaning of life's deepest mysteries with such a divine combination as this.

And so Alyssa had, nearly every night for the past week, in all the best pubs and restaurants Ireland had to offer. She just couldn't get enough of the Banoffee Pie.

God, really, she just couldn't get enough of this.

Tucking her purse firmly under her arm (she was in a public house, after all, and not stupid), Alyssa leaned back and closed her eyes, letting the sounds wash over her in a delightful jumble. In all her thirty years of life, she'd never quite encountered anything like it. Lively Irish reels on the fiddle, banjo, and guitar from the impromptu "jam session" in the corner warred with the loud, almost incomprehensible chatter (or good craic, as the Irish called it) from the locals on all sides.

It was perfect, and Alyssa was determined to memorize every detail. She wasn't sure how she was going to recreate it in Fáilte, back home in Seattle, but by God she was going to try.

She'd have to hire live musicians, for sure, and… Alyssa whipped out the notebook she'd pocketed for just these moments, and wrote down her observations and a note to ask Aunt Mary about costs. She was about to cap her pen and order another Bailey's — just one more drop — when her cell rang.

She frowned, but she quickly left the pub to answer it. For Aunt Mary to call her from the States in the middle of Alyssa's "research" trip, when they had been functioning just fine via email, it was going to be either fantastic news, or very, very bad.

"Hey, sweetie," Aunt Mary's voice sounded tired and old, something that only happened once in a million years.

Very bad, then. At least Alyssa could trust her business partner to tell it to her straight.

And so she did. "We're in serious trouble. We may need to close Fáilte."

Two hours and a few good cries later, Alyssa wandered back into the pub and ordered a whiskey on the rocks. "Sláinte. My life's hell," she muttered, and promptly forgot all the rules about not getting drunk alone.

"It's a sorry excuse for a blow-in you are, and no mistake," piped a voice at her elbow several drinks later.

It belonged to a very short man with a friendly, wrinkled face and a jaunty air. By now, Alyssa was used to Irishmen approaching her in bars, especially since she was not only a single female tourist, but an attractive blond one at that. This guy just didn't strike her as the flirtatious type, however. He looked like he ought to be a leprechaun, although he was wearing the same tweed attire as most of the locals, and Alyssa instantly liked him.

He slid her a fresh Bailey's and settled himself in for a long talk. "Tell auld Cory all about it, love, and I'll do me best to cheer ye up, 'ey?"

Her current drink definitely had a salty edge to the usual boozy creaminess. She gladly accepted the replacement the tiny man — Cory, was it? — had offered her.

And was simply unable to hold it together anymore. "I'm losing my pub at home because we're having so much financial trouble and I love it so much," she wailed, "and I was s'posed to be here in Ireland to research gourmet food like at Avoca or Ballymaloe to take the pub up a notch instead of down and now I have to cut my trip short and go home and lose everything and…and it just sucks!"

"Sure now, lass," Cory murmured soothingly, and his hand on her shoulder was warm and comforting. "There's a story to make a grown man weep, there is. I tell ye what, I know just the thing."

He lowered his voice conspiratorially, and Alyssa leaned in closer. He was so sweet, and somehow she just knew she could trust him. "It's the greatest treasure of all Erin, and — oh, I'll say no more just yet. Drink up now, 'ey? Sláinte!"

"Sláinte," Alyssa agreed, and tossed her drink back.

☙

Stupid.

Stupid, stupid, stupid.

You'd think, with all the guidebooks Alyssa had read beforehand, there would be no way in hell she'd ever find herself in her B&B room with no recollection whatsoever of the previous night and a strange, squat black pot-looking thing sitting in the middle of her floor...

Although now that she thought about it, none of her guidebooks had ever mentioned the danger of acquiring black pot-looking things while drunk.

Or the porridge, for that matter.

She was sure she would have noticed if a guidebook had warned her against accepting gifts of porridge while under the influence. It was still steaming, right there in the pot.

At least she still appeared to have all her clothes on. Her purse was untouched, too. "Thank God for small mercies," she mumbled, her head pounding horribly. Whatever she'd done last night, she didn't even want to know. She'd gotten off lucky, even if she couldn't figure out the porridge.

Maybe the nice hosts had sent it up — she'd probably forgotten to lock her door, she should see to that — when they saw she was in no state to come down to breakfast. She didn't even know what time it was now.

Her stomach gurgled, and she eyed the hot cereal speculatively.

It smelled delicious, and the more she thought about it, the more sure she was her B&B hosts had delivered it. Maybe they were just really into rustic presentation. "Better eat it before it goes cold, right?" she grunted to herself, and discovered it was quite possibly the best she'd ever tasted.

The pot was a lot larger than it looked from the outside. No matter how much Alyssa ate — and she ate way more than she meant to — it hardly showed any signs of decreasing.

Nifty trick. She really needed to stop before she threw up…only come to think of it, she didn't feel sick at all. Still, ashamed though she was that her appetite couldn't match her hosts' generosity, she reached down to return the pot to its owners — and a slip of paper fell from the bottom.

It appeared to be torn from a page of her own notebook, but the handwriting was definitely not hers, being rather flamboyant and scrawling. In case young Alyssa forgot already, it read, this be the Cauldron of the Dagda and a gift of the Good Folk of Erin. Use it wisely, and the blessings of the Irish be upon ye!

It was signed 'Cory.' "Huh," she said aloud into the room. Apparently 'young Alyssa' had indeed forgotten already.

"Huh," she said again, a few minutes later after doing a web search for 'Cauldron of Dagda.'

If this was the same as the one from Irish folklore, she needed to do some rethinking about the nature of reality.

According to the internet, it was a cauldron of plenty, created by the minor deities/head fairies/whatever the hell the Tuatha dé Danann were, from which "no company ever went away unsatisfied." She looked back at the pot. It'd be stupid to try to work out the physics of the thing, right?

And she was either having a very vivid hallucination — complete with full belly — or she was going to have to admit there were things on heaven and earth she had not yet dreamed of.

Her watch beeped, and she jumped and looked down at it guiltily. Crap — she needed to be out of her room in ten minutes. She'd have to worry about this mystery later, especially now that the pot was conveniently empty (!) and ready to be packed away in her luggage.

Weird as hell.

But already she had to admit she was getting some ideas for what to do with it. She still couldn't remember how she got it or who this

"Cory" was, really, and that was worrying and all, but this could be… this could be the key to saving Fáilte!

⌁

Three days later and safely home at last, Alyssa was beginning to wonder if taking the Cauldron back to Washington State had been such a good idea.

It had held her up waaaay too long at customs — apparently it jammed (jammed!) the scanners or something and she'd been delayed for hours while she demonstrated that it was just a quaint little tourist item for which she must've lost the receipt or something and it had been a HUGE mess but it was too late to go back with it, so there you go.

Aunt Mary had looked askance at it too, when they'd been unpacking Alyssa's stuff in their shared condominium. "Call it whatever you like, sweetie," she'd said dubiously, turning it this way and that in her hands, "but I don't think it was really worth all that hassle. We've got a lot more important things to worry about. Now, we've gotten an offer on the business…" and so on.

Alyssa decided to leave out all the bit about the Good Folk and the never-ending food supply. Aunt Mary wouldn't get it, and even if she did, she didn't have the imagination to use it for Fáilte's benefit. Probably.

But Alyssa would definitely have to approach the matter carefully, so she tried a different tack after she'd looked over all the numbers with her aunt. "Look, Aunt Mary, I'm the co-owner, right? Let me do some research about…about lowering our costs for supplies and things, and I'll punch up some of our recipes with the stuff I learned on the trip, and we'll see if we can't pull into the black in the next couple of months."

She added a note of pleading to her voice, knowing the woman would be powerless to resist. "Please, please let me give this a try — I don't want to throw away all the work we've put into this place!"

It worked. "Oh, all right," Aunt Mary smiled and ruffled Alyssa's hair. "If anyone can pull it out of this mess, I guess it's probably you. You've always been the creative one."

And that, as some are wont to say, was that. Alyssa promptly shooed her aunt out of her bedroom and shut the door, whistling a jaunty reel as she sat down on the floor for some quality time with this great mystery.

It was too bad that Magical Artifacts didn't come with manuals like food processors or something. She now heartily wished she hadn't been so drunk the night she acquired it…maybe Cory had explained everything to her then and she'd just forgotten. How, for example, did it know when there was a need for food or not? Could it be sort of… programmed to spit out whatever she wanted?

No, she discovered very quickly. No, it could not.

In fact, it seemed to have an internal menu that had very little to do with the time of day or her dietary preferences, for the next time she felt her tummy rumble (aha! Apparently hunger was the trigger!) the pot filled to the brim with…something.

Something unrecognizable and truly disgusting to look at — some form of meat, perhaps? — in a watery yellowish liquid that really just reminded her of urine and smelled distinctly sharp and unpleasant.

"Oh, hell no!" Alyssa glared at the Cauldron for a full ten minutes, willing it to change to something else — it steamed innocently back at her — before she did the unthinkable and sampled a tiny bite of the whatever-it-was.

The oily slick on the pale meat got all over her fingers, and she had to plug her nose and close her eyes before she could pop it into her mouth without gagging. It was absolutely nasty, and at the same time remarkably satisfying, and she caught herself reaching for another piece.

"Not okay at all," she muttered, and went to do another internet search.

Her squawk of indignation almost brought Aunt Mary to the door. "Hare boiled in rancid butter? Who the hell comes up with these things? No no," she called through the door to her aunt's concerned noises, "I just got a funny email, no worries," and resisted the urge to bash her head against the wall.

The Cauldron was stuck in the culinary Dark Ages.

So much for a gourmet rotating menu at Fáilte.

Not about to give up on her scheme just yet, Alyssa hauled the pot over to the pub kitchen the next morning (after it had thoughtfully provided her with black pudding — ew! — for breakfast). Maybe while surrounded by all sorts of modern Irish culinary delights, it would get a clue by osmosis and start producing stuff she could work with.

In the meantime, she went ahead and added Banoffee Pie and some other delicious new recipes to Fáilte's menu, and started working on a marketing plan for the new "surprise menu."

If she worded it right, she'd get them curious. Then, provided the pot didn't always gift her with blood pudding or rancid rabbits, she could have a 'surprise! authentic Irish food of the day' thing or somesuch.

See? She'd still salvage this with a little creativity.

⌗

Her plan worked, sort of.

As in, she was able to fit in many of the Cauldron's medieval offerings over the course of the first week. Some things she didn't dare put out in the menu, even though she knew the magical properties seemed to render everything mildly addictive. (She still caught herself eating the hare on occasion, disgustingly enough.)

Other offerings could be incorporated into her already existing menu, such as the various interesting cheeses or stew items. Even better, more people were dropping in for the 'Surprise Menu' and even saying they 'just couldn't stay away' — and since she never ran out of those items, the food costs didn't rise with the additional custom.

The stupid Cauldron never did catch on to the fact that it was operating in the 21st century, though. Hell, it didn't even yield any potato products. Apparently the Tuatha De didn't believe in the New World.

Oh, Alyssa tried everything — dropping the Banoffee Pie into the Cauldron (the poor dessert just got rancid butter all over it), trying to assemble ingredients in the pot when it was in its empty state (that resulted in the magical, food-related equivalent of a plumbing disaster, and she never tried it again), even reading recipes aloud to the pot when no-one was around.

Nothing worked at all, and she started feeling positively weird after mucking around with the thing all day — almost like reality was wavering around her.

Magical Artifact, right.

Maybe she'd try again next week.

Only the next week, she had other problems to deal with, starting right in on Monday.

"At least let us do the sous-chef bits for you, Aly!" That was second-in-command Gina, standing with feet planted and arms crossed in front of Alyssa's locked workroom where the Cauldron was waiting for her to start up her day. "It's got to be crazy for you in there, doing it all yourself. It's not normal for the owner — or the head chef, for that matter — to take on that much work, you know."

"I like cooking. I like having my secrets, too — secret recipes, I mean." Shit. She should have known someone was going to nose in sooner or later. Trust ever-helpful Gina to be the first trouble. "Just like on the ad, right? Plus I am a professional. Have I ever looked like I was swamped or anything back here?"

"Well, no, but —"

"Then don't worry about it! I, uh, learned a lot of new stuff while I was over in Ireland, you know? So I'm just working on that stuff, practicing new techniques —"

"But why aren't you teaching them to us like the other recipes? I mean, the Banoffee Pie is a house favorite now, but I've had reports that people are even addicted to your special black pudding! Or the Irish oatmeal, for crying out loud! You can trust your staff with those secrets, don't you think?"

This was getting awfully tricky. "Ye-es, but I — you know what? I'd just rather do this myself for the time being. It's what I want to do, all right? You take care of the rest and don't worry about me." Alyssa hated taking that sharp tone, but she couldn't think of a better argument than "because I said so" just then.

Of course she couldn't tell them the truth or anything. They were already wondering where she kept getting all the weird cheeses.

Further argument was interrupted by the strangest sound Alyssa had ever heard coming from the tiny wine cellar at the back of the building.

If she strained her ears, it seemed to be…singing.

Yes. A male voice singing Irish folk songs. Although it certainly wasn't professional band music, but rather the sort of off-key, wandering sound that was an offense to her ears. "Do we have a drunk in the back alleyway?" She asked Gina with a raised eyebrow.

"I can go check, but I think it's coming from the wine cellar. Do you think Rob left his music in there or something?"

Alyssa couldn't think why, but she went ahead and checked anyway. The music stopped as soon as she opened the door, so that ruled out the iPod theory…but she couldn't see any signs of disturbance or evidence that anyone was there.

"Hello?" She called, glancing around the room. It was a small space, and although there were plenty of dusty crates and boxes lying around, surely there was no place for a person to hide?

Just to make sure, Alyssa checked every nook and cranny, even looking behind the wine rack.

Which was when she noticed something was missing.

There! She knew she had four bottles of the mélange noir out on the rack last night, and now there were only three. But what that had to do with the singing was anyone's guess.

Further searching revealed the empty bottle stowed behind a stack of crates. How on earth had anyone gotten into the cellar, drunk a bottle, and escaped without anyone noticing? Alyssa admitted she'd been holed up in her workroom for unhealthy amounts of time, but surely Gina or one of the others would have noticed…unless they were the culprit…but what about the singing?

Thinking about it made Alyssa's head hurt.

It seemed more like something one of those Irish fairies would do than anything else…

Wait a minute. She'd done some searches on the Good Folk and the Sidhe and so on while she was looking at the Cauldron online, and something did seem familiar.

"It was actually my phone," she told Gina as she re-emerged. "Must've fallen out of my pocket while I was in there. I have some weird music on it." She only hoped the little bastard in there — whatever it was — wouldn't start singing again and ruin her perfectly plausible story.

In the meantime, she did some quick searches and decided to test some things. A saucer of milk? No — maybe a small glass of wine. Maybe she could lure it out or something.

This was ridiculous. Here she was, researching Irish fairies and trying to figure the best way to catch one. Had she completely lost her grip on reality?

"Let's face it, Alyssa, you lost that when you took home an artifact of the Tuatha Dé Danann," she muttered, and set out a little cup of her favorite wine anyway.

The next day — Tuesday — one of her kitchen helpers quit, and couldn't even give her a good reason why. Alyssa was so busy helping Aunt Mary deal with that that she didn't even think about the whatsit in the wine cellar.

She did hear the fry-cook accuse Rob the dishwasher/errand boy of snitching food off of some of the plates ready to go out, and she made a mental note to keep an eye on him and see if he was really the cause of the cellar trouble after all. But she had her hands full with the cauldron anyway, which had given her a nice, meaty Irish stew when she already had one set up on the regular menu. Now that was a headache and a half.

On Wednesday, she heard the singing again while she was hastily adding Cauldron cheese to some onion tarts, and knew Rob hadn't been anywhere near the cellar. This time, she approached it quietly, listening carefully to the sound, as much as it grated upon her poor ears.

It was definitely in a thick brogue of some kind, reminiscent of that fellow Cory only a bit more tinny.

Holding her breath, she eased open the door very slightly and peered around it.

The music stopped abruptly again, but she was rewarded with a flash of red — like a little peaked cap — before the cellar was still. She was betting anything it was a Clurichaun, according to her research.

Little drunken pixie thing that guards the wine-cellar? Just about as plausible as a Cauldron of Plenty, really.

Maybe she'd somehow transported the one with the other, all unknowing. At least poor Rob was off the hook as long as she left a little wine for the creature.

That was Wednesday.

On Thursday, another kitchen helper quit, also refusing to say why, and Alyssa started to tear her hair out.

The marketing had been working beautifully — or maybe it was the Cauldron food itself — and demand was higher than it had ever been before, so she really could have used the help.

The Cauldron started doing extra duty as she figured out ways to store some of the staples like cheese and salted meats for later use in other recipes, but even with its help in cooking time for things like stew and porridge, she had to work twice as hard now.

On Friday, the fry-cook demanded that Alyssa fire Rob or he'd quit. Apparently food was still vanishing off plates from the regular menu all week (although never the Special stuff) and the fry-cook was convinced it was the boy. Alyssa had expected the problem to stop when she appeased the clurichaun — the wine-bottles, at least, were no longer vanishing — but maybe she was wrong.

With a heavy heart, she had to fire Rob despite his protests of innocence, promising to hire him back if his name was cleared.

In the meantime, she overheard some of the servers muttering about the weird lights in the bathrooms and found herself doing another load of research.

Demand for the Special menu rose to extremes over the next week, and although the Cauldron never failed to supply, Alyssa had to admit she was getting creeped out. Patrons she had once thought perfectly normal were behaving a bit like rabid animals, or like druggies coming in for their daily fix, and she started eyeing the Cauldron with some worry. There's been no mention of addiction in the old legends she looked up.

Not that she was going to get rid of it or anything.

Fáilte's business was soaring despite the problems, and already Aunt Mary's eyes lit up whenever she looked at the numbers. Alyssa was just going to have to do more research, that was all. She wasn't going to let things get out of hand.

Then two weeks later, all hell broke loose.

It was a Saturday. It started favorably enough, with a bustling morning business (they'd just expanded their hours) that never really seemed to go away. By lunchtime, people were arriving in droves. Alyssa had stopped bothering with marketing because word-of-mouth seemed to be doing just fine, with more people coming in every day.

She had new trainees in the kitchen and on the wait-staff, so maybe that was the reason everything seemed to suddenly start going wrong.

Customers started complaining about uneven portion sizes — some people were getting much more than others even though the cooks swore they were going out the same — and people kept on having 'incidents' in the bathroom, emerging dripping and bewildered and babbling about 'weird lights.' Tempers were beginning to run short by the afternoon, and Alyssa gritted her teeth and prepared for a hell of a day.

But when the goat suddenly appeared and started a riot, she admitted she wasn't nearly as prepared as she had thought.

Alyssa was holed up again in her little cave, ladling stew into a massive pot and totally not trying to hide from the chaos, when the screams started. As she tore into the dining area, heart hammering, she began to hear words amid the shrieks.

"What the hell is that?"

"Is that a freaking goat?"

"MANAGER!"

And so on. The source of the shrieks was readily apparent in the form of a white goat that was dashing here and there among the customers, destruction following in its wake. It looked kind of panicked, and she didn't blame it.

How on earth had it gotten there?

No time to worry about that now. Gritting her teeth, Alyssa waded into the throng after the poor creature, trying to make herself heard over the cacophony to get the patrons to stop scaring it. Her words had absolutely no effect.

Especially when a man burst from the restroom completely dripping, bellowing that the toilet had tried to drown him.

Now there was no reasoning with anyone.

Tables and chairs crashed to the floor, along with all the nice food, dishes, and many bottles of booze, and everyone was rushing for the available exits in a blind panic.

All Alyssa could do now was watch it all collapse. Her beautiful pub… her reputation…

Was that a horse?

Yes, yes it was.

She couldn't see the goat anymore, but that was definitely a full-sized white horse in the middle of the room now, snorting and stamping as the very last of the patrons — and staff — struggled out the doors in terror.

It didn't look…normal, and when it rolled its eyes toward her, the only person left in the room, she suddenly knew: it was a phouka, yet another fairy creature of Ireland that had no place in her poor little pub in America.

She couldn't remember: was it supposed to be benevolent, or would it just as soon eat her?

She snatched a broken bottle from the floor and brandished it by the neck, just in case.

"Well, that is quite enough of that."

The voice was deep and smooth as a movie actor's, and it came from behind her.

Alyssa spun, and there were two tall, beautiful…people standing in the doorway to the kitchen as if they'd been there all along. The man had long black hair and one of those perfect faces straight out of a smutty romance cover, and was dressed in something Alyssa could only describe as Lordly. The woman had even longer hair, thick and blood-red, and a long gown of shimmering green, and her face was also inhumanly beautiful.

They both looked faintly disapproving, and Alyssa suddenly felt the urge to throw herself down on the ground and kiss their feet or something equally stupid.

"Um, hi," she said instead. And, "You're probably the Tuatha dé Danann, aren't you?"

Their frowns deepened. "How dare you take what was rightfully ours?" the Lady's voice was cold and pure as a bell. Alyssa found herself gaping like a fish.

"We have protected the Jewels of our people for centuries. You, a mortal, came into our Sidhe and stole one of our precious artifacts. It has taken us far too long to find you, and the very fabric of the veil between our worlds has been dangerously warped. Have you anything to say?"

She finally found her voice. "Take?" she sputtered. "Look, I didn't steal anything, ok? I don't know what you mean about jewels, but Cory gave the cauldron to me as a gift. Short guy, wrinkled face, uh." She couldn't picture his face now, couldn't really describe him to save her life.

But she did suddenly remember a little bit of that drunken night now — the dark all around, and a hill that opened like a door and Cory leading her in…

It occurred to Alyssa that she'd been had.

The Lord and Lady looked at each other. "Cory," murmured the woman. "Perhaps Corb?"

"Or any of the other tricksters who wish to disturb our careful work. This is just the sort of havoc the fear daerg would try to wreak." He gestured around the utterly destroyed pub, having apparently forgotten

Alyssa existed. She whipped around again, suddenly remembering the huge horse, but there was only a small white dog there now, which trotted up to the Lady and wagged its tail.

Not too bad, then. Could have been a lot worse.

Which reminded her. "I think there's a will-o'-the-wisp in the men's room," she said, her shoulders sagging. What a mess, and all because she'd gotten drunk and let a strange little man give her a gift to save her pub.

So much for that.

The Lord raised his head and gazed off into space for a moment. "And a Clurichaun, and a few others besides," he said, showing no emotion she could see. "I think we'll be taking them all with us now." The Lady snapped her fingers at the now-docile Phouka, and glided back into the kitchens.

"Wait," Alyssa said desperately, "what about my pub?"

The Lord looked at her impassively. "What about it?"

"Well — I mean, it's not my fault it's been destroyed like this, is it? I never would have stolen that pot from you — and it's caused enough trouble I don't even want it now — but it was one of your people that did this to me, right?"

The Lord simply looked at her.

She hunched her shoulders. She had to try, didn't she? Fáilte was her life. It was a little piece of her favorite place in all the world.

Well, damn.

And she was going to have a hell of a time explaining this to Aunt Mary. A goat somehow got in and everyone panicked? Not that there was any way they'd be able to keep the pub open now...

The voice of the Lord broke into her thoughts. "What on earth is that?"

The Lady had removed the Cauldron from its place in Alyssa's workroom, and both of them were looking into it.

Alyssa dared to peer over their shoulders, and stared at the contents for a very long while.

Then she began to giggle uncontrollably.

Then she started weeping at the same time.

She should have expected something like this.

"It's Banoffee Pie. It's goddamn Banoffee Pie, and your stupid piece of Dark Ages shit just now figured it out. Fucking hell."

Giving everything up for lost, Alyssa handed forks to the Tuatha dé Danann and sagged down onto her hard little chair, alternating between gasps of laughter and tears.

The Lord and Lady obviously didn't get the irony, but they certainly understood the allure of the Banoffee Pie.

"I have never had mortal food like this before," the Lady said wonderingly, looking at the way the chocolate dripped off the fork.

It was warm as if straight from the oven, and smelled absolutely magical.

The whipped cream was beautifully swirled, and the short biscuit on bottom was a perfect golden brown.

Alyssa couldn't have made it better herself, and she knew the toffee was going to be exactly the right amount of sweetness for the luscious bananas without even taking a bite. She could almost feel the Lady's sigh of pleasure as she placed it on her tongue.

"This is…truly delicious," the Lord said. He looked vaguely bemused.

"Yup. The wonders of modern Irish — well, technically British — cuisine. You should get out more. I have been trying to train your stupid pot to make it for two weeks, did you know that? It must be a slow learner." She didn't even bother hiding the bitterness in her voice.

They finally drew away from the pot and looked at her. Their joint gaze made her knees knock.

"Perhaps our Cauldron needs a little updating. The other Tuatha Dé might appreciate it," the Lady said to the Lord. He nodded.

"It has been a long time since we have ventured from our Sidhe to the mortal realms. We cannot stay here in your country long, for it warps the nature of the Veil between our world and yours. Come back with us to our hills, and we will reward you richly."

Alyssa froze. She tried to think. "As a sort of consultant or something? I dunno, there are probably plenty of —"

Wait, what was she saying? This was her one chance to fix everything!

"I'll take it, if you promise to help my Aunt get this pub back on its feet. You've got fairy blessings or something, right?"

"We are *not* fairies." The Lord looked thunderous, and Alyssa paled a little. "But it will be as you say. To thank you for the...Banoffee Pie, was it?...we will bless your pub a thousand times over. Your aunt will still need to rebuild what has been broken, and you will no longer have our Cauldron, but I promise you that won't matter in the slightest. Your business will soar, your food will satisfy like no other, and your public house will be spoken of in every home. Will that do?"

Alyssa thought about it, and grimaced. If the Lord meant that literally, that could be a serious problem. "Maybe not every home. I don't think we could handle that volume of business. Just a little blessing to get us back on our feet would be fine. But can I have some time to explain things to my aunt?"

The Lord and Lady nodded. "A year and a day, in your time. We shall expect you in Eire. Then we will find you."

They opened their mouths and called something in Gaelic, and a ball of light shot into the room, followed by a tiny fellow in a red cap, and something Alyssa thought might be invisible.

"One more thing!" She was probably crossing a line now, but she just couldn't help it. They were about to leave, after all.

She gestured to the pot.

"Can I at least have the pie?"

⊕ END ⊕

(Not a) Fairy Tale

This was one of the very first stories I wrote — that is, I actually completed — when I decided to "get serious about writing" after college. Originally created for a YA workshop challenge with the theme "First Dates" (did I put some of my own awkward high school outcast feelings into this story? Yes. Yes, I did), it ended up going in a weirder, more magical direction. It's what I do. (The workshop, by the way, approved.)

Side note: the retro ice-cream parlor in the first scene is basically lifted from one in my hometown. I used to go there as a child, and I'm pleased to say it's still there, and thriving!

For the first time in my life, everything was going perfectly.

There I was, sitting on the very edge of my shiny red vinyl seat, gazing in awe and wonderment at the extravagant confection the waiter placed in front of me.

Perfectly round scoops of vanilla-bean ice-cream, a mountain of fresh whipped cream with lashings of chopped nuts, the entire thing lavishly drizzled with hot fudge sauce…with those things alone, the sundae would have been pretty close to heaven, but it was the strawberries that pushed it over the edge.

It wasn't just because it was the beginning of berry season in the Skagit Valley, ensuring the most luscious, ripe fruit imaginable (although it helped), or that strawberries were my all-time favorite sweet thing ever (they totally were).

It was the sheer romance of it. Mom always said the strawberry was the most passionate of fruit, and looking at the deep red, juicy slices artfully arranged on the dessert I had to agree. They were even kind of shaped like hearts.

I wondered if Derek had noticed this.

Oh right, because I'd almost forgotten the best part of all — the fact that I was going to share this fabulous, romantic dessert with guy. A really cute guy. Because we were on an honest-to-God first date, complete with retro ice-cream parlor (it was even done up in Valentine-y red and white, candy-stripes and curlicues galore) — the perfect place for the first romance of my life.

I glanced up at Derek finally, trying to keep the cheesy grin on my face from looking too idiotic. Act casual, right. "Looks pretty good, huh?"

"Mmm." He stared at it absentmindedly, then leaned back and looked at me, chewing on his lip kind of anxiously.

Since I didn't know how to read that at all, I took up my spoon and carved out a perfect first bite.

And promptly choked on it with my date's very next words:

"So Cyg, have you ever considered that you might be a fairy?"

So much for a perfect, normal date.

I'll be honest, as a pick-up line it kind of fell flat.

As a statement in earnest, which apparently it was — judging from the way Derek was looking at me across the sundae — it was completely unexpected.

I swallowed hastily and put down my spoon. "A…fairy. Like, wings, magic, bippity boppity boo?" He couldn't possibly have known about my addiction to fairytales, right? I'd kept that well away from my school life — I was weird enough as it was; I didn't need extra mockery fodder.

Besides, Derek Wingfield wasn't one of the mean ones at Rainy

Valley High. He was one of the clever, funny, nice ones. Really cute, too — I mentioned that, right? — had the whole dark-haired poet-type thing going, without being nerdy about it.

And apparently, despite being a knowledgeable, mature Senior to my less-knowledgeable Junior, he was in deadly earnest about the fairy thing. "Seriously, Cyg. I mean, I know I sound like a total dork, but hear me out! I know this guy who does paranormal research, see, and…you think I'm crazy."

Well, yeah. But I wanted to give him the benefit of the doubt. He was the first guy to ever actually ask me — me! — on a date, so there was no way I was going to ruin it.

All the same, this was not at all how I had envisioned my first date going.

The first part of it had been fun, if nerve-wracking: the movie was one of those crowd-pleasing action flicks with plenty of explosions which gave us something to talk about over dinner, which was pizza so I didn't have to worry about fumbling with silverware while my hands were all sweaty, so bonus points to Derek for that.

The conversation hadn't been too bad, either, and I had been very careful not to mention any of the weird stuff about me — like the fairytales, or the fact that I play Dungeons & Dragons with my cousins every weekend.

But seriously, what guy asks his date if she might be a mythological creature? Where the heck did that come from?

At least he'd waited until most of the ice-cream parlor patrons were gone for the evening.

I took another spoonful of chocolate-smothered dessert and pretended to savor it while I tried to think of something to say. "Just promise me this isn't going to be a clever build up to a really cheesy punch-line and —" I narrowed my eyes. "Is this about my name or something? 'Cause I've had enough teasing over that to last a lifetime."

"I don't think Cygnet Pemberton is that weird of a name," he said hastily. "Cygnets are young swans, did you know that? That can't be all bad, right? Swans are beautiful, and, um, so are you." He turned pretty red at that, but I could feel my face heating up too, only probably worse.

Still, I could stand to hear a bit more about that, and a bit less about fairies.

I sighed and put down my spoon again, dragging my hand through my hair without thinking. I could feel it spring out of its pins immediately, and cursed. So much for all that work to keep my frizzy mane under control. I resisted the urge to race to the bathroom to check the damage. Some things were more important than unruly hair, right?

Like not insulting my perfect date when he was saying perfectly ridiculous things.

"I did know that, about the swan thing," I said, trying to stay cool about his little compliment. I took a deep breath, and hurried in. "But see, the problem with your theory is that I'm most decidedly not a fairy. I have two very human parents and a birth certificate to prove it. I think they would have noticed if I was switched at birth or something, and most importantly, I am pretty sure fairies don't exist."

There, that summed it up pretty well, although everyone knew Mom was incredibly beautiful, in an almost unearthly way. It was kind of depressing, actually.

"Okay, but for a moment just pretend fairies do exist."

God, he wasn't going to let this go, was he? I guess there could have been worse subjects to beat to death, but I was beginning to feel embarrassed for the both of us.

And I was tired of that feeling, these days.

Too many weird things had been happening to me this year, at school especially.

Like this last Tuesday, the day Derek asked me out. I mean, that part was beyond awesome, but the rest of the day had been pretty strange.

So I'd been wearing a short peasant skirt my mom had given me, a camouflage tank top, and my tall lace-up boots (that didn't even match). I liked the weirdness of the look, but I was pretty sure it missed trendy by a mile.

But the entire day I kept getting compliments right and left, from friends, enemies, and people I didn't even know. Even some creepy College Guys whistled in the mall after school.

And the thing is, I could have sworn I wore basically the same thing only a week before that and got my usual dose of ignoring/casual insults from the popular crowd. My hair was the same frizzy red-gold halo as always, and my very pale legs still knobby at the knees, far as I knew.

I mean, at my best I was pretty odd-looking, with the whiter-than-white skin and the crazy hair, which I supposed were the fault of my Irish granny, and the pale green almond-shaped eyes — I had no clue where those came from. So what was with the one day where everyone seemed to think I was gorgeous?

Now that I thought about it, the same thing had happened a few times before, about a month back.

I hadn't been wearing anything special those times, either. It was like some switch had turned on, and then off again for everyone but me, and the first time I thought it was one of those cruel tricks teenagers — especially girls — will play on the unpopular ones. But it would have to be pretty sophisticated to get the College Guys in on it, right?

I had apparently been musing over this too long, for Derek was clearing his throat. My ice-cream had melted into a chocolatey soup, so I guess I'd been staring at it for a long time instead of responding...

I tried to remember what he had been saying. "Fairies. Ok. So if they exist, what's your evidence? Do I have invisible wings or something?

Magical powers I haven't noticed? Fae Glamour?" Dammit, I was giggling. But he didn't look insulted — in fact, he looked impressed.

"You know about that part, then? The glamour thing? I read all about it in this guy's guidebook. I think you have it sometimes."

Ha. "What, like last Tuesday?"

"Exactly!" He looked relieved, and I finally started to think he really believed this stuff he was saying to me. I still had no idea where he was going with it.

Then it was like a light clicked on in my head. "Wait a minute, are you saying you asked me out because I glamorized you or something?" I almost clapped my hand over my mouth. I hadn't meant to ask that out loud — I didn't really want to know if that's what he thought I'd done.

But it was too late to take back now.

He looked suddenly really uncomfortable, and that was more of an answer than I needed.

It would figure that only time I get a hot date, he'd want to back out of it by claiming I used fairy wiles or something.

The hardest thing was that almost I started to believe him. How else would you explain all the weird other stuff? Maybe I had made him do it on accident.

I was not going to cry. "I…I think we're done here," I said, and rose from the table. "I'm sorry, this is too much for me. Maybe —"

Derek rose too, and quickly grabbed my hand. "Cyg, look," he said, and kissed me. Right there in the ice-cream parlor in front of everyone.

It was just a light kiss, and technically the only other person in the parlor was some guy with a newspaper, but it still rooted me to the spot. Suddenly I had no idea what that meant. Had I made him do that? Did he still like me? What was supposed to happen now?

"Uh." I said, intelligently.

He was talking very fast now, and had gone quite red again. "I don't want you to get the wrong idea, Cyg. I like you, ok? I mean, I did feel kinda weirdly compelled to ask you out but I'm really glad I did. You're really funny, and smart, and didn't even blow me off when I mentioned the fairy thing, so…um. Don't write me off or anything? Please?"

He was cute when he groveled.

And I wasn't mad at him or anything, I just didn't know what to think. "Ok," I said, and smiled, and thought about maybe kissing him back. The guy with the newspaper started coughing and hacking up a lung, and I jumped — I'd forgotten we weren't totally alone. "So maybe we should go somewhere else and talk some more?"

"Yeah — yeah, let's do that." He looked nervously at Newspaper Guy and hurried us out the door.

I tried a joke. "I didn't think I could use my fairy magic on him if he kicked it, sorry." He seemed distracted, but then he grinned back.

"So are you saying you believe me now?"

"I'm almost 100% sure I'm not a — y'know, with my parents being normal and everything — but I guess it's true that something's weird about me."

"Well, I was thinking more like in the blood or something. I guess I should've said that. Maybe you have fae ancestry, is what I mean."

That made a bit more sense. As much as this whole thing could make sense. "Either way, it's kind of far out there. But I dunno, there's no scientific reason for the glamour thing and it's too weird to be a fluke, so until something better comes along, I guess there's worse things to be than quasi-fae."

There. I hadn't exactly said I believed him, but I guess it was pretty obvious I did.

⊹

Because the next day, the whole school knew that weirdo Cygnet Pemberton thought she was a fairy.

"So are you like, Tinkerbell, or something?" That was snub-nosed

Kensie Hanson, who loudly asked me about it after the first class of the morning. When there were plenty of people gathered around our lockers, of course.

"What?"

"Well, I have it on good authority that you're a pixie, or something like that. Or at least you told Derek Wingfield you were!" She burst into sniggers, and the others around followed suit.

"Crazy," someone else said.

"I — I never said that!" Tears of rage started to build in my eyes. How could he?

I'd honestly thought he believed it himself — I mean, he'd been the one to convince me, not the other way around! But to go spreading around lies now, like this — I should have known last night was too good to be true.

The trouble was, I couldn't find Derek all morning. And everywhere I went, the whispers followed.

I was going to go down in School History as the crazy chick who thought she was a fairy, and nothing I could say would make any difference. Way to ruin the rest of my high school career, and with only my Senior year to go, too.

What's more, it probably meant the glamour thing really had been an elaborate joke and Derek had been in on it.

Someone must've seen me with one of my beloved books and hatched a scheme to ruin my life. Then they'd gotten the whole school to pretend I was really gorgeous, on set days, and even gone the extra mile to bribe some random strangers outside of the school to fool me further.

And then when the time was ripe, Derek — the school's best convincer — would swoop in and supply the finishing move, and then spread the word.

I had been the butt of a school-wide joke that was months in the making.

⊷

Except it was even worse than that, because it was on video.

No wonder my denials were going unheard. Seemed like everyone by lunchtime had seen a very incriminating set of clips from the ice-cream parlor — cut together in the worst possible way — that really did make it seem like I was confessing my fairyhood to Derek. Now I was well and truly pissed, like I had never been before.

All the other little mockeries were kid stuff compared to this.

It was time to fight back.

The air seemed kind of bright and misty around me when I finally saw Derek down the long hall, trying to sneak to his next class without seeing anybody. No way was I going to let him get away. A crowd started gathering around me as I tore down the hall, some of them gaping openly.

Yeah, yeah. They wanted a scene? I guessed they were going to get it.

"You!" I said furiously before he could duck into the classroom. "Don't you dare move!" He froze like a deer caught in the headlights, his eyes wide with terror. I would have felt sorry for him if he weren't such a bastard, he looked so small and miserable. Standing before him now, I actually felt kind of taller. More powerful.

"Cyg, listen —"

"No, you listen, you miserable rat! I —" The crowd around us was still gaping openmouthed, and I realized I was in no mood for an audience after all. "Go away," I snapped, and as one, they slunk away. The entire mass of high-schoolers, even pug-nosed Kensie.

Even one of the teachers that had been passing by.

I must've looked even scarier than usual or something.

I caught myself staring bemusedly into the sudden void in the hallway — I'd never imagined it could be so silent.

Into it broke Derek's voice. "I didn't make the video. They've been hassling me all day too, ok? Maybe we should talk about this later, when you're not — uh — glowing like that."

"I am not glowing!" I wasn't going to fall for stupid tricks again. Except now he had completely distracted me from what I was going to say to him.

I took a deep breath. "Ok. You have five minutes before class. Convince me you're not a rat-bastard."

He actually looked kind of haunted. "So I wasn't lying when I thought you had something, ok? I did ask you out without thinking. Then Trey and Hannah and some of the others caught wind of it and said they would make my life a living hell if I didn't play along with their little scheme. So I was supposed to convince you about the fairy thing, and Trey would be in the same room to make sure I did it."

The hacking guy with the newspaper. I clenched my fists, but Derek plowed on. "Only by the end of it, I didn't want to anymore, because you were really nice and I…I mean, I kind of started to believe what I was saying, ok? So I told them it was off, that I didn't care what they did to me, I wasn't going to back them up. I didn't know they got video."

The tang of blood was in my mouth and I realized I had bitten the inside of my cheek. I wasn't surprised Trey Maddox or Hannah Oliver would be the ringleaders – Trey hated me ever since I owned him in debate and Hannah was probably jealous that Derek even asked me out (since apparently they hadn't bribed him to do that) and everyone knew she wanted him.

But it couldn't have been just them.

"How many? Who else was involved?" It was nice (or weird?) that he seemed to think I still had fairy glamour or something, but I wasn't buying any of it.

I needed real answers, and either Derek was almost as clueless as I was or he was really good at being cagey, and I was running out of time right now.

"Look, you find some way to get them together after school where I can talk to them," I snapped, since the bell was already sounding for the next class. "Use whatever excuse you like. I'll be waiting behind the gym."

"O-kay." He looked dazed, but I had the feeling he was going to do it.

I had never felt so in control before.

I still wasn't done deciding if I hated him or felt sorry for him, but one thing was clear: neither he, nor anyone else, had any power over me right now.

The bright, misty feeling didn't go away for the remainder of my afternoon classes, and I didn't even care that everyone was staring at me pretty much nonstop.

I scarcely noticed that no one had even tried to tease me to my face; I was too busy thinking about after school. I wasn't exactly sure what I was going to say to Trey or Hannah or whoever else had done this to me, but I was sure I would find a way to make them grovel, make them admit what they did in front of the whole school, prove I wasn't crazy...well, it might be too late for that.

And if it turned out the whole school had been behind it from day one?

Some inner part of me whimpered at that thought. No one likes to be made a fool, especially on that grand a scale. It was much easier to believe I really did have fairy glamour than to think about how completely I they might have hoodwinked me.

But I'd deal with that when I knew for sure. Somehow I'd deal.

It was raining when classes finally let out, but I headed straight for the fence behind the gym anyway. I was used to the rain; it was part of living in the Pacific Northwest, even with summer just around the corner.

I welcomed the cold, letting it settle into my bones as the rain plastered my clothes to me. It suited my mood; let the others gather underneath the shelter like pansies.

Through the rain I could hear them coming. There was Trey's deep rumble: "This had better be a really good bribe, Derek, because we're not letting you off the hook for pocket change."

Hannah's high-pitched whine: "Why do we have to meet out here in the rain, anyway? Is this like a drug deal or some — Oh. You." They all stopped beneath the overhang and stared at me.

Ok, I guess it was pretty weird for me to be standing in the pouring rain with my arms crossed, but even Derek was gaping and he'd known I was going to be there.

There were four of them with Derek: Trey and Hannah and Kensie (no surprises there) and some cheerleader-type chick I'd never even spoken to before, I think her name was Breanna or something.

That kind of stung, and I couldn't think of anything to say for a second or two.

"What're you doing here?" Hannah sneered, recovering more quickly than me. Derek had already managed to vanish into the rain but the others hadn't noticed. "You can't get us to shut up about the video or anything, you know, it's all over school already."

Now that we were down to it, I didn't even know where to begin. I could feel pinpricks of tears at the corners of my eyes, but the rain at least would hide that. "You put Derek up to it. You made him try to trick me into saying something stupid for your stupid camera, and even then you had to twist everything I said, you stupid toad. All of you. Toads."

Trey laughed, but it sounded a little bit nervous. "So what if we did? You're still bat-shit crazy, am I right?" That was directed to his cronies, but they seemed distracted. Breanna was whispering something to Kensie and I caught the phrase "glowing again."

Distracted, I looked down at myself but I couldn't see any difference, except that everything was still hazy.

They were playing tricks on me again, obviously. How stupid was I to keep falling for it?

I had to stay on track. "So did you — what, get the whole school to act really weird around me last Tuesday to set me up for this?"

They looked kind of confused. "Tuesday?" Breanna asked. "Isn't that the day Derek — oof." Hannah had elbowed her in the stomach, but didn't look any less bewildered than Breanna. Well, maybe it had been all in my head from the start.

Maybe I was just as crazy as they said I was.

That was no reason to let them get away with spreading the stupid "fairy" thing all over the school.

I wished Derek had stuck around, though. I wasn't sure how I felt about him, but either way he should've been here for this.

I took a deep breath, and stepped forward. The rain had stopped and now the sun was out and my clothes were steaming slightly. I must've looked kind of freaky, because they all took a step back as I moved. They were practically cowering, and if I squinted my eyes, they almost looked a little bit toadlike. Encouraged by this, I straightened and glared at each of them.

"Yeah, you'd better be afraid. I'm not crazy, and I certainly don't think I'm a fairy. But you're probably right that it's too late to go around and tell everyone you set me up and took that stupid video out of context, because the damage is already done.

"So I guess I'll just have to make you pay for it." I leaned forward, feeling energized all of a sudden. It was as if I really did have some sort of magical power, the way they were all reacting to me.

They were actually afraid of me.

Suddenly I didn't like it. "I'm done talking to you," I said abruptly. "Don't try this shit again. I'm not going to take it from anyone anymore." I turned and left, and as I went I noticed the bright haze was fading around my eyes.

I didn't really feel tall or powerful anymore, but…something had changed.

So I probably wasn't a fairy or anything. So what? I could face down the popular kids just fine on my own, and I had a feeling those four weren't ever going to bother me again.

Behind me, I heard the faint sounds of croaking.

↢ END ↣

THEY STOLE MY LOVE LAST NIGHT

I wrote this story late in 2016, the first of two new short stories created specifically for my mother. At the same time, I also had been invited to participate in a short story bundle with a "Haunted" theme. I didn't particularly want to write a ghost story; when they're not scary, they're always so sad, so full of regret. And I had been in the habit of writing dark and sad stories for the past year. So this time I decided to create a challenge for myself: a ghost story with an ending that would make us both happy.

The story also features something dear to both our hearts: a hauntingly beautiful Celtic song that played at my wedding. (Alasdair Fraser plays a stunning version you can find in his album "The Road North.") Finally, the White Skye Inn is an homage to one of our favorite hotels in the world: Hotel Eilean Iarmain on the Isle of Skye.

Please understand: this is not my story.

(Although for my part in it, I have no regrets.)

Where to begin?

Ah, the Isle of Skye. Of course. Everything begins and ends there, at the White Skye Inn.

∾

First, let me tell you about the rain.

Imagine:

It's late spring, and the rain drums all around us, a steady, iron-gray blanket that obscures my vision from the backseat of our taxi. I can only assume it is also the reason for the excruciatingly slow progress we are making on the country road. 'We' includes myself, my grandmother Marie, and our taciturn taxi driver, whose name I don't know and haven't thought to ask.

The silence is heavy on our heads in this moment; beside me, Granmarie grips her purse in her lap, her wrinkled hands white at the knuckles, her face pale. She stares straight ahead, seeing only whatever images — memories, ghosts? — are playing inside her head. She's grown progressively quieter as we finish the last leg of our journey through Scotland: from tour-guide vivacity, to wistful nostalgia, to silent introspection.

I can't know exactly her thoughts, but you can be certain they center around Grandpa Mac and his death ten years ago. Here, on this very road; perhaps in weather just like this.

The rain picks up its tattoo on the roof of the taxi, on the windows, on our psyches. As the gravel crunches and our driver pulls into the courtyard of White Skye Inn, I can't make out a single detail to touch my childhood memories of the place. The curtain of gray is too thick.

The rain is important, you see, because of what comes next.

Once we're stopped, I flip the hood of my coat up and stumble out into the mud and the downpour. Our driver, still silent, goes for our bags, and I go for Granmarie. My insides are a churning mess of emotions, running the gamut from anticipation and nostalgia for my favorite childhood holiday place, to annoyance at the rain, to deep worry — or perhaps even dread — for Granmarie, who hasn't said a word since we crossed the bridge to Skye.

This trip is all for her, and I'm beginning to wonder if it's a mistake.

I open her door on the other side and muster a cheery smile for her as I offer my arm. "All right, Granmarie?" Her eyes are glistening with tears as she turns her head up toward me, and I swallow a sudden lump in my throat.

"I'm all right, Jessamyn. Or I will be soon." She breathes deep, then reaches out a hand for support and puts a foot on the cobbles.

All at once, the rain stops.

From downpour to nothing in the space of seconds. It takes me a moment for the realization to sink in; Granmarie also pauses, her hand still clutching my arm. In the sudden silence I can hear the call of gulls over the loch, the hiss of waves on the rocky beach behind us.

We look up, and there is a perfect blue hole above us. Clouds on all sides, but none above the White Skye Inn. I feel the midmorning sun on my face.

For a hushed moment, everything seems to go still. I breathe in the earthy green smell of the damp ground. A faint thread of melody teases at me, achingly lovely and melancholy. I look around, but can't find its source. Tears still glimmer in Granmarie's eyes, but she is smiling.

I wonder: is this a sign?

❧

Wait.

Perhaps my part of the story begins here, when the rain stops.

But for Marie Jones McAllister, it begins much further back.

❧

It's 1969.

A young up-and-coming classical violist, one of the only women in her class, is touring internationally with her college's elite chamber orchestra. It's her first time out of the States and she's eager to experience everything Europe has to offer, so while they're on the final leg of their tour in Glasgow, she and some of her friends decide to attend a 'traditional music session' at a local pub on a whim. Marie Jones is always up for music and drinks, even if she doesn't really know what 'traditional music' means in this context.

She's about to find out, and her life will never be the same.

The pub is pleasantly crowded, and on any other night Marie would be looking at her options, maybe hoping to use a little flip of her brunette curls and a gamine smile to win her some free drinks and fun conversation.

But not tonight, for the moment she walks in the door, her entire attention is completely arrested by the little stage — well, not much more than an area cleared of tables — at one end of the room.

A young man with a violin and an older man with a guitar play something fast, toe-tapping, and utterly beguiling. The young man's bow dances on the strings — that's right, she remembers, when you play it like that, it's a fiddle, not a violin — and she can't take her eyes off him. He's grinning, his fingers flying, his foot stomping to the music. People around her are whooping and whistling, and she finds herself joining in as the boy swoops in for one last, bright flourish.

He has a very attractive smile, she notices.

He bends his head to confer with the guitarist. He grabs a swig from the drink on a stool beside him, and announces, "A bit of a change of pace, here. Something for the fairies." Marie could swear he's looking at her.

He puts the bow to the strings, pauses, closes his eyes.

A sweet, clear note sings out, then another — a minor key, the tempo slow, but lilting. The conversation quiets to a murmur.

The melody is more than sweet, or sad. It's haunting, aching, reaching into every part of her. Tears gather in her eyes by the first refrain. And the young man on the stage sways in place, his body moving as one with the music.

Marie watches his face and realizes he feels it every bit as much as she does — every hushed fall, every heart-piercing rise. He's doing this for the love of it. He's doing it because he can't not play this music.

The guitar accompaniment is deft, changing the lovely harmonies and chord structures beneath the fiddle so that every time the melody repeats, a new dimension of the tune is revealed. But something is missing, Marie thinks.

There should be a second instrument dipping and soaring with the fiddle, weaving a harmony below that beautiful, melancholy tune. She can hear it in her head; perhaps something a bit lower…something that could reach into deeper, duskier notes than a fiddle could, but still blend tone for tone.

She imagines herself, viola in hand, making sweet harmonies beside this man, and finds her heart unaccountably fluttering, her cheeks growing warm.

She wonders who she can find to teach her fiddle…on a viola.

～⊷～

White Skye Inn is just as I remember it, I decide as we gather our bags and pay for the taxi. The hush brought on by the sudden weather change has been broken already by our driver starting to whistle cheerfully while moving our final pieces of luggage to the side. It seems the sun has brightened his mood, too.

The sun has brightened everything. The old whitewashed stone buildings gleam, their sage-green doors and roofing providing a muted echo of the rain-drenched, rich green showing through the garden gate to our immediate left. To my right, between two buildings I can see a bit of the loch, sparkling up close…and still stormy in the distance.

I shake my head in wonderment, but am quickly distracted by Granmarie's hand on my arm. I'm about to ask her what she needs from me, but I stop, because her face says it all. "Oh, Jess," she whispers. "It hasn't changed a bit."

She's looking at the garden gate, and for a moment her eyes widen, and her breath catches.

I don't know what she sees, but she's squeezed her eyes shut now, swaying slightly in place. Her hand still clutches my arm.

Just then, a cheerful shout comes from the direction of the main house. We turn, and there's my great uncle Jack and his son, William, coming toward us with big grins on their faces. And there's Jennie is in the doorway, waving. The family of Grandpa Mac.

I look sideways at Granmarie, who has been avoiding White Skye Inn for ten years, to see if she's as prepared for this as she said she'd be. She dashes tears from her eyes and holds out her arms with a smile, I think of genuine delight.

We've always liked the McAllister side of the family.

Just not quite enough to come back to the place where Grandpa Mac died.

Until now.

There's hugging and smiles all around, the usual 'how was your trip' 'oh, great, except for the weather' 'and how's college life, Jess' 'So excited to be finishing that math degree next year' and 'how's the family' 'they were fine last time I checked,' and so on. They relieve me of all the luggage I've been trying to handle, and we follow them to the main house. I send one glance back toward the garden gate, wondering again what Granmarie saw. And I catch her looking back as well.

At the question in my eyes, she simply shakes her head.

↜

Marie Jones comes home from that fateful Europe tour and embarks on a mission.

(She never has her chance to speak to the attractive young fiddler from the pub, as the session goes much later than her friends are willing to stay. But she does get a name from the bartender before they leave: Duncan McAllister.)

The music still lingers in her head long after she has returned to the States.

Her mission is threefold: One: Learn how to fiddle on a viola. Two: Find the name of that haunting song, and learn it. Three: Find Duncan McAllister. Somehow.

Not one of these tasks promises to be easy.

Her family, much more interested in having a world-class classical violist to brag about than a fiddler who doesn't even play an actual fiddle, is not supportive of her new goals. Of course she doesn't tell them about number three. In fact, she stops telling them about her fiddle lessons or the fact that she's been spending countless hours adapting tunes for the slightly lower register of the viola.

She continues to play in the symphony in college and get decent enough grades in everything else that her parents will continue to fund her. She dates boys and enjoys herself. But she's busy expanding her network of Celtic musician friends, saving up to go to Nova Scotia or somewhere she can get in on the traditional music scene.

She gets better and better, because Duncan McAllister or not, she wants the music. It enchants and enthralls her. She doesn't have a drop of Celtic blood — probably — but she has this music in her soul, and she wants more.

A year later, she gets her chance to go to a real Celtic music school for the summer.

The name of one of the instructors? Duncan McAllister.

⌁

Practically the second thing the McAllisters ask us about is music. They've settled us into a suite overlooking part of the 'garden,' which I now remember turns into a beautiful tangled wilderness once you get beyond the first set of bluebell-lined paths. I'm eager to explore it again. I was eleven the last time I was here, and I still have magic-filled dreams about that wild, green place. But I don't have an opportunity to go there right away, because Uncle Will has found Granmarie's viola.

"Oh, Marie, I thought you had given it up for good! You don't know how happy this makes me. You don't know how it saddened our hearts to hear you had stopped playing."

The silence goes a bit too long. I look at Granmarie to see the impact of his words, but she is busying herself with something in her bag. I don't know how to tell him that yes, she started playing again last year, but classical pieces only. She still hasn't touched a single fiddle tune. Although her fingers are in excellent shape for a nearly-seventy-year-old, they aren't as fast as they used to be.

More importantly, I'm not sure her heart wants to go there again.

I, too, long for Granmarie to go back to the way she was, but I have always hoped that, much like this trip to lay Grandpa Mac's memory to rest, the music will come when she's ready.

"And I hear you play the double bass these days, Jess?" Uncle Will finally says, and I jump on it with relief.

"As a hobby, like my mother with her cello. I'm nowhere near a McAllister level." I smile self-deprecatingly. But he latches onto the thread, and we chat about my occasional gigs with various groups — Celtic, Jazz, you name it, I like being eclectic — and how yeah, I've done some fun "bottom line" duets with Mom a few times but we're both too busy to see each other much right now.

Which is a half-truth, because Mom and I don't really want to see each other right now. But this isn't about me. I'm here to help my Granmarie, because no one else on my side of the family will. And even though I think the McAllister side is on our side — Granmarie's and mine — I feel like I don't know them very well, after ten years away and limited correspondence.

So I leave it at that. For now.

Before we leave to join the rest of the family, I look one more time out of the window at the verdant rain-soaked green of the garden. Soon, I think. Then something catches my eye.

I'm not sure what I am seeing. A person, I think at first. But then I think it's just a wisp of mist.

Only...there's no reason for mist to form up in the wilds of the garden, nor for it to be shaped like that. Shaped like...

My heart stutters for a moment.

"What do you see, Jess?" Granmarie's voice has an odd quality to it. One I find hard to interpret. I shake my head.

"I don't know. Nothing." Maybe it's just steam, perhaps rising up from some sun-warmed rain puddle. Maybe my mind wants to see things it will never see again.

Like Grandpa Mac.

His presence here is strong here at the Inn, metaphorically speaking. Too many memories lurking in every corner. I know Granmarie can feel it too. "Just wishful thinking," I say, partially under my breath.

I turn to see Granmarie looking at me intently. She opens her mouth, but Uncle Will calls for us from the stairs. Food is on the table.

"What? What is it?" I ask her as we head out the door, but she shakes her head.

"Later," she half-whispers.

For the second time today, worry creeps into my heart.

⌁

It's the first session of the Celtic Arts Workshop, and Marie is determined to behave naturally with a certain instructor — for it is, indeed, the same young man who made her fall in love with fiddling. Marie doesn't believe in fate, as such.

But she does believe in making the most of this opportunity she's worked so hard to get.

She knows she's an unusual addition to the group of musicians. She's not the only violist who's ever taken up fiddling, but her insistence on sticking with the viola instead of getting a new, proper fiddle is more unusual. And much more difficult. She has to learn tunes by ear or spend time transposing them. She works on harmonies to anchor the fiddles during group sessions, but some purists dislike harmony on the fast tunes. Playing an octave lower means killer string crossings, but she is determined to master them all.

She learns to work through all these things, insisting on the viola every step of the way. Because its darker, full-throated tone has always been her first love. Because she thinks it has something to offer Scottish music. And because someday she wants to play that haunting tune from the Glasgow pub. Preferably with someone…

And thus her current state of affairs. How to approach him?

Reluctantly, she concludes she must, above all things, behave like an adult. And a student.

After the first session, held in one of the campground areas by the main lodge, she musters her courage. There are other girls like her approaching him. Young women with stars in their eyes. He's handsome, and charming, and plays like a young god. Of course they will be all over him.

But she knows what she wants to say, and she'll say it with no expectations of the outcome.

"I saw you play in Glasgow," she says, once it's her turn to talk to him. "It changed my life. I'd never heard music like that before. It's why I'm here, doing this."

The smile that breaks over his face nearly stops her heart. "That's wonderful, that is! You're our sole violist, right? I love your spirit. And you clearly know your way around that instrument."

He's noticed her already. She desperately hopes it's not her mistakes he remembers. "I'm classically-trained, but fiddling is very different," she says hesitantly.

He becomes serious. "Don't give up, now. You're doing something different and fresh here. You'll have to work harder than most everyone here, but I can promise it will pay off. I see it in you."

She finds herself blushing very hard.

He grins again, and reaches out to flick her hair. "I'd love to hear you play a classical piece sometime. Bet you'll play circles around me."

She suddenly laughs. "Bet I will!"

She wants to ask him about the song, but someone else approaches him. He catches her eye before she leaves, and says, "I look forward to talking to you more, viola lass."

I need to tell him my name next time, she thinks.

She gets her opportunity the next day, after the initial whirlwind settles down. He beats her to it, though, when she comes up to him.

"Marie, right? I'm learning names today." His smile still has the same effect on her knees, but she holds herself together.

"I wanted to ask you about a song," she says, "a specific one I heard once. You played it, actually, in Glasgow. It won't leave my head, but I don't know its name."

His face changes, from friendly to genuinely interested. "A mystery! Come sit down," he offers, and pats a log. "Can you play the tune, or hum it for me?"

She's tried many times to pick the tune out on the viola, to no avail. Even now, she only has vague memories of how it made her feel.

"I don't think I can," she admits. "It was very beautiful and sad. A minor key, and," she suddenly remembers, "it was a strathspey." She's learned the name of that stately, slow-but-lilting tempo by now.

He shakes his head. "I play a lot of minor strathspeys. They happen to be favorites of mine." He ducks his head as if he's admitting to some great folly.

"Mine too," she says, smiling. "But I haven't heard this one again. I am sure I would recognize it. It got me, right here." She puts her hand over her heart, and notices him watching her with more interest than she's seen before.

"Then I'll just have to play minor strathspeys for you until we find it," he announces suddenly, and goes for his fiddle.

She can barely contain her glee.

⊸

I don't get Granmarie alone until hours later.

After a late lunch, Uncle Jack and Aunt Jenny offer to give us a tour of the Inn so we can see what's new, and we accept. But Granmarie asks for the garden to be left alone — she wants to get reacquainted on her own, explore it for herself. There's a strange inward look on her face when she says this, and because I knew she would be quiet and introspective on this part of the trip, I try not to worry too much.

But the truth is, I want to do the same thing myself. Something about the garden has been calling me since the moment the rain stopped. And I know I didn't…see what I thought I saw from the window, but all the same, I know I will have to go there soon. If only to reassure my own mind.

The tour reassures us that less has changed at the White Skye than our relations think. Sure, some interiors of the outer cabins — converted from a grand old stables back in the day — have a brand new shine to them. The roofs have been redone, and there are sturdy, fine new benches on the lawn overlooking the sea loch.

I approve of the updates, but I still cherish all the old familiar things.

The weathered stone steps leading toward the loch overlook, the hand-lettered signs painted right onto the sides of the buildings, the round turret that connects the main building to the quaint little pub… where Grandpa Mac would always play.

Oh, yes, there are shades of him everywhere. Every time we come to another place rife with memory, I look at Granmarie and hope. I hope this trip will be everything we wanted it to be. I hope she can find that last piece she needs to finally heal.

What I see on her face is merely puzzling.

I'm anxious to get her alone so we can talk.

It's late afternoon when we find ourselves alone. Granmarie has requested her time in the garden, and Aunt Jenny has smiled and left her to it. I stand outside the main building, wondering if I should go inside as well, or ask her to talk first.

But she solves my quandary by taking my arm. "Walk with me, Jess," she says quietly, and leads us to the garden gate.

"But I thought you wanted to go alone," I protest.

"It's different with you," she says simply, and my heart warms.

My mother says I spend too much time wanting to be a good granddaughter. She also says that I love nothing more than solving people's problems, just like the math major I am.

But the truth is, I want to be there for Granmarie because she understands me, and I understand her. And she lets me help her, which no one else in my family does.

And for moments like this.

We enter the garden together.

The sunlight has taken on that warm honey glow of the late afternoon. The clouds continue to avoid our little corner of the island, and while I find it bemusing, I certainly prefer this to the pouring rain. Puddles have still collected in the cobbles of the walkway, and the earth beneath the shrubbery is dark and rich with moisture.

The garden is at once strange, and familiar.

The part nearest the entrance has been redone, with paving stones on the pathways and pretty, orderly arrangements of the flower beds. But there is a second gate, and we are both drawn to it without speaking.

I find myself humming under my breath. It's the same faint piece of melody that came into my head earlier, but I can't remember why I know it or what it is. I can only assume it was one of Grandpa Mac's tunes. It's beautiful and sad.

Before we open the second gate — to the wilder, greener woods beyond — Granmarie suddenly stops and turns to me.

"What's that you're singing?"

I blink. "I'm — not sure. It's just stuck in my head."

"So you've been hearing it too," she whispers. She looks ahead, into the trees, then back at me. "Jessamyn, what did you see in the window earlier today?"

"I — I don't really know." Even though I've wanted to get Granmarie alone, it's so I can talk to her about all the strangeness in her face and try to find out how she's truly doing. Not talk about the strangeness I've been experiencing.

But the way she asks the question tells me that maybe the two conversations are one and the same.

I swallow. "Granmarie, why are you asking?"

She shifts and rests her hand on the wrought-iron gate, closing her eyes for a moment. She lets out a breath. "Because I've been hearing things. Ever since I started playing music again. I felt…compelled, somehow, to come back here. And now I'm seeing things too."

Somehow, I have known from the beginning that this is what she will say. And I don't know how to respond.

Because there is no logic in this.

I shake my head, and push open the gate. I'm not running away from the conversation, I tell myself. I am looking for answers.

"I saw mist, or steam," I finally say. "Maybe smoke. It was out here in the woods."

I step through, and hold the gate open for her. Then I kick myself, because I am doing this wrong. I am not being a good granddaughter. "But Granmarie, what did you see?"

I know what her answer will be.

"Duncan," she says.

⌒

For three days, Duncan comes up with new strathspeys to play for Marie during their breaks. Every last one of them is beautiful, sometimes to the point of tears. But she is certain not one of them is the song she wants.

Finally, on the third day, she has an epiphany: "I just remembered! You said this one was for the fairies, when you announced it. Does that mean something to you?"

She remembers that particular phrase, because she had been so certain he was looking at her when he said it.

"Ah," he says softly. "I wondered."

He wondered, but didn't play it for her earlier?

Suddenly Marie has a few things to wonder about, too.

He starts to play, and Marie feels it like a sweet knife to her heart. It's the song. A lump forms in her throat, and her hand goes her mouth. She nods, not sure she can speak, and he plays it the whole way through. Softly at first, and then soaring. With no accompaniment, it sounds different, but she doesn't want it to stop.

"Lass," he says when it's over, "You chose the one song I don't know the name to."

She wipes the tears from her eyes, and asks him to teach it to her anyway.

Marie doesn't know this yet, but this is the moment that Duncan begins to fall for her.

After the workshop is over, Duncan decides to stay in the country for an extra week. Just to keep seeing Marie, as he admits to her later, when they are no longer teacher and student.

Long before the week is over, he asks her on a date. She says yes.

๑

So. Granmarie has been seeing Grandpa Mac again. Here, in the garden woods.

And so have I.

She's been hearing a melody, aching and bittersweet.

I've been hearing the same one.

I try to argue myself into reason. If one person has a song trapped in their head, they often unconsciously hum or sing it. Then someone else, hearing this melody without really realizing it, will get it stuck in their head too. That would make sense. Logical sense.

But as for the other thing…

There's really only one way to know for certain.

"Granmarie," I say slowly, trying to think like a person who solves problems. "We have to figure out what's going on. We have to test this somehow."

I can't help but feel that the answers we want are here, in the wild part of the garden. The green woods. The bracken and bluebells and wild rhododendron.

The reason for the excitement fizzing in my veins.

And some fear, too.

We venture further in. The paths here are not much more than swathes cut into the tall grass and bracken, or beaten into the earth by many feet before us. The McAllister's like it wild out here.

In places, the trees hang over the path, meeting each other in what I used to call "fairy arches" when I was younger. As if they were doorways into a magical kingdom. Their limbs twine together, and the light filters through them, amber-gold in the late afternoon, or early evening. The air is sweet. I find that I am holding my breath as I move beneath the arched branches.

I am certain that something will happen here. But what, I don't know.

Granmarie leans on my arm, not because she needs the physical support, but because she is feeling it too. She is feeling…something.

"Duncan took me here," she says softly. "We had only just gotten engaged. He took me to visit his family, and because he wanted me to play a duet with him. He said he wanted us to play for the fairies."

I've heard this story from Granmarie before. It took a long time for her to want to speak about her Duncan again, after…everything. But a few years ago, when I proved to be a good listening ear, she started telling me the stories. About music, about travel, about Duncan.

And whatever is unexplainable thing is happening at White Skye now, I want to be here for her. So even though I've heard this story, I give her my full attention.

"Jessamyn, we played the song. The one I've been hearing in my head." She starts to hum, and I find myself joining in.

Then a third voice joins us: a voice of a fiddle, sweet and ethereal.

Our eyes widen. I quickly scan the area, but see no one. I can't even pinpoint the source of the music.

But we both hear it, and it's not just in our heads.

I do the next logical thing. "Who's out there?" I yell.

I receive no response, but for some reason, I don't expect one.

The music fades away again, leaving the rustling of leaves. Faint memory tugs at my mind, of being in this place, in a moment much like this. And the feeling of something magical. The feeling that something is about to happen.

I catch movement in the corner of my eye, but when I turn my head I see nothing. "Granmarie," I whisper, "What happened that day, when you and Duncan played for the fairies?"

She's looking into the woods, one hand clasping the other. "We talked, first. He told me the name of the song at last. He'd finally tracked it down, just for me…" She frowns, and I'm not sure sure why she's paused. Simply remembering, perhaps. "Then, we played. We played it low and sad, and high and clear…just like we'd practiced. I wove my harmonies with his melody, and the other way around, too. And then…" she trails off. "I don't remember. Something wonderful. Something magical."

Again something tickles the back of my mind. Something I've forgotten. I close my eyes, trying to chase it down.

"Oh Jess, look," Granmarie whispers.

The urgency in her voice makes my eyes pop open. I follow her pointing finger.

Between the trees, under one of the 'fairy arches' of my childhood, a misty figure stands. Holding a misty violin and bow. And I know him.

Of course I know him.

"Duncan," Granmarie says hoarsely. "Duncan, why are you here?"

Grandpa Mac's figure points his wispy bow toward my Granmarie, then holds out his fiddle toward her.

Her hands on her mouth, she takes a step toward him, then another. He vanishes.

A sound breaks free from her: half gasp, half sob. I rush to her side and put my arms around her, but I don't know what to do. How to solve this.

I feel a sudden spark of anger. How dare he — or this place, or whatever, whoever is responsible — torment her like this? What are they — or he, or it — trying to do?

"Granmarie," I say tightly, "Here's what I think. I think we need to either solve this —" I gesture to the woods around us, to the arch where Grandpa Mac stood moments before — "Or we need to go home."

The grasp of Granmarie's hand over mine is tight, perhaps desperate. "I think he — I think this place is trying to tell me something. Help me, Jess. I don't know where to start."

The light is falling. I catch more motion in my peripheral vision again. Simply the movement of birds flitting between trees? It's hard to say.

But I feel like I am missing something important. "Maybe we need time to think," I say. "We should come back tomorrow. Jack and Jenny and all will be wanting us in for supper soon, anyway, right?"

"Perhaps," she says, and her eyes are faraway again when I turn to look at her.

We turn and head back toward the White Skye, although neither of us is able to resist looking back over our shoulders the entire way.

"Granmarie," I ask as we reach the gate again, "What was the name of that song?" Maybe it's just curiosity. Maybe it's because I think it might be significant. I'm not sure.

Granmarie pauses, perhaps gathering her thoughts back again. "The song…Duncan taught it to me the first time we met, you know, but he didn't know the name then. He had learned it from his father as 'the song about the fairies.'"

The story sounds familiar, but not enough to jog my memory.

"But when he brought me here to the woods with our instruments, he told me he had finally tracked down the name of the song. I remember. He said his father probably hadn't told him because it sounded so funny. So…different from the way the music makes you feel. It was called 'They Stole My Wife Last Night.'"

I have a difficult time sorting through my emotions. How very odd. It's true, the name doesn't fit with the tune. It must be from Celtic folklore, I realize.

Both the Scots and the Irish believe fairies are neither good nor evil, but mischievous, dangerous. And sometimes these mysterious Folk steal people, for reasons all their own.

Combined with the sad, aching tone of the melody, the thought gives me the chills.

Yet there must be a reason this song has been playing in our heads. And surely it must be connected to the…to everything.

As we put the garden behind us for the remainder of the night, I start trying to wrap my head around the impossible.

⁘

In the early 70's, the whirlwind romance between Marie Jones and Duncan McAllister continues across continents, to the dismay of her family and the delight of his. He proposes to her after six months, then whisks her out to his family's property in Skye, where they run a generations-old bed-and-breakfast.

Their first day there, he takes her to the garden, and they play together.

'For the fairies,' Duncan says.

Just as if it were a strange and wonderful dream, Mary can't remember everything about that day — only that it is important.

She falls in love with White Skye Inn. She and Duncan live there for several years while their joint music career blossoms. They begin to be sought-after for their unique duet style, and are invited to play all over the world. They don't have a lot of money, but they do get to travel.

And between every tour, they go back to the White Skye Inn. For family, for local music sessions, and to play for the fairies.

Marie gives birth to Stella Aileen McAllister. She and Duncan are pressured by the Jones side of the family to bring the baby home to live in the States; they compromise by living nine months in the Midwest, and three months in Skye, until Stella is old enough to go off to college and doesn't need them at home anymore.

Then Marie and Duncan go right back to touring, and back to the White Skye Inn.

They visit Stella during breaks, sometimes, and bring her out to them for summer vacations. But when Stella meets Rob Silver, gets married in Colorado, and starts having kids of her own, her annual trips to Skye dwindle to a mere week every summer. Although she does bring her children each year, to the delight of all the whole McAllister clan.

Then, when the oldest of the four Silver children — a certain girl named Jessamyn — is only eleven years old, the trips stop. Abruptly and permanently.

The tragic road accident only claims one life, that stormy day, but it is the one man whose music and laughter has held everyone together.

And the family mourns Duncan McAllister, but no one more than his wife, whose life revolved around the songs they wove together.

Marie Jones McAllister leaves Skye behind and moves back to the States with Stella.

She puts away her viola, because it only reminds her of what she's lost. She finds a job with a travel agency, booking tours for other people. She doesn't touch the music — any music — again.

Not until nine years later, which is perhaps where this story should have started all along.

Because that's when her dead husband starts calling to her from across the sea.

⌁

By the next day, I've put more and more of the pieces together. Granmarie has helped me.

I think I know what we need to do.

I just have to convince her to do it.

"I don't think I can, Jess. It's been so long. I'll sound bad." I also hear what she's not saying. *I'm not ready to unlock that side of me again.*

Because of course the answer is her music. She and I both know she will have to play that song in the garden. She'll have to play Celtic music again.

I don't know what will happen next, but that much I do know.

"I'll be there with you, if you want," I offer.

She's silent for a minute, thinking it over. "Maybe you should play with me," she says.

I'm taken aback. This moment, this entire thing from start to finish, isn't about me. What place do I have in that garden, except as support?

But then, that's the role I would play with my instrument anyway. The support.

"If the family has a double bass on hand, I could try," I say at last.

When I leave the suite, I turn back to see her take the viola out of the case. She tucks it under her chin and closes her eyes, but sets the bow firmly on the desk beside her. Her left hand begins to run the fingering silently. I understand. She's willing, but not quite ready to actually set the bow to the strings yet.

I find Aunt Jenny, and ask her if there is a double bass on hand for sessions at the pub and other get-togethers. As I've suspected, there is. Jenny's face lights up at the prospect of hearing me play, but falls slightly when I tell her it's for a private session in the garden with Granmarie. For the healing process.

"The garden is a good spot for that," she says, smiling. "Sometimes I think there is more to that place than meets the eye."

I wonder what she and Jack and Will would think if I told them everything. But I'm not ready to take that kind of risk.

As we head to one of the spare rooms where the instrument is stored, Aunt Jenny catches my arm. "See if you can convince your grandma to come stay with us, won't you? I mean, to live here again. We always loved having her and Duncan here, and not just for their music. I told her that, but I don't know if she is willing. I just —" she falters here. "Not to speak badly of your mother, of course, but…"

"Granmarie isn't happy living with her," I finish for her. I've been thinking about this a lot. I think Mom resents Granmarie for choosing the music first. Even if it's not what Marie intended, when she and Duncan moved back to their old ways the moment Stella left for college, I think that was the message that my mother got.

In response my mother got married, settled into a home, had four kids, and stayed put.

And then what did Granmarie do, but come running back when she lost Duncan?

Stella loves Marie. She took her in without a second thought. But there's resentment there. I'm familiar with it too.

Suddenly I wonder if I've been making things worse myself, by spending so much time with Granmarie instead of my own mother.

I shake the thought from my mind as I haul out the old bass. "I'll talk to her, " I promise Jenny. But I don't think it will work, and part of me selfishly doesn't want it to.

Regardless, I remind myself, the future hinges on what Granmarie and I are about to do.

⤝

The garden is green and gold in the early-afternoon sun, the air sweet. The blue hole in the sky above us continues to hold.

It has taken us a while to gather our courage and make our way here. Plenty of reasons to stall presented themselves — eating brunch, looking up the song online (for me), and practicing fingering (for both of us) because we want to be perfect.

But we don't play anything. Not yet.

In the hush, the stillness among the tangled trees, I strain to hear… something. The song, or some clue as to what we should do next. Sudden doubt grips me.

Looking at Granmarie, I see that it grips us both.

We've carried our instruments out with us. I tuck the bow of my double bass into my back pocket and stand up tall, leaning the old instrument's bulk against my body. I place one hand on the fingerboard, one ready to pluck the strings, and look at her, because we need to do this together, no matter how much my heart is hammering.

The way Duncan and Marie arranged it, the song is supposed to begin with the melody of the fiddle, joined by the harmony in the next verse, the bass plucking notes beneath. But there is no ghostly fiddle to start us out. It seems we must call it — and call him — to us.

Granmarie's hands shake slightly as she lifts her viola and bow into place, but she nods at me. She closes her eyes, and plays one low note, then another. She's playing the melody an octave lower, and I nod my agreement with her choice. What better way to invite the higher fiddle to join us, without sacrificing that haunting melody?

I begin to pluck my notes beneath, a simple, soft bassline that mostly serves to bolster her if she needs it.

But scarce moments later, the sweet, sweet sound of Duncan's fiddle pierces the air above the two of us, and I forget anything else.

My breath catches, and my fingers stumble. Granmarie's dusky viola notes falter, then strengthen, as she dips into the harmonies of her past.

And there he is.

It's unmistakably Grandpa Mac as I last saw him. Suspenders, wild mane of hair, fiddle in hand…and playing as if there is nothing else in the world.

And behind the misty figure of my grandfather, soft light — green and gold and blue —builds within a tangled arch of intertwining trees. Like a doorway into something else. Something…

Suddenly, I remember.

Memories from my childhood. From the garden beyond the garden.

Seeing things I couldn't explain…

I stop plucking the bassline. The viola and violin are soaring together; they don't need me anymore. And I've lost the thread anyway.

Because…

They're real. The fairies are real.

And they're here. They dance around the edges of my vision as the song rises and falls. They weave among the trees. Shimmers in the air, colored lights, never quite in focus. Through the archway I can make out more shapes, tall and short, graceful and gnarled and strange. Clouds of hair that seems to move on its own, gossamer wings, skin brown and rough like a tree. All of these things and more — so much, in fact, that my mind can't comprehend it.

Their voices are like whispers I can't quite make out.

But like planets and the sun, my attention — and that of the fairies — is drawn to and circles around the pair of them. Marie and Duncan. Lovers reunited.

Or are they?

In all the lore, fairies are tricky creatures. Untrustworthy. Their morals are not human morals.

I don't know what I am truly seeing: Duncan' ghost, or an illusion created for some dangerous, treacherous purpose?

The song ends with one last, beautiful note. It seems that we all hold our breath.

The ghost speaks.

"Marie. My viola lass," he says, and his voice cracks with emotion. It sounds no different from when he was alive. Despite my misgivings, tears fill my eyes and a lump forms in my throat. I couldn't speak up now even if I wanted to.

"Duncan —" Granmarie's voice breaks too. "Why are you here? What is this?"

He sets the misty violin and bow down on a mossy stump. I resist the urge to go and touch it. To see if it's real.

Grandpa Mac reaches out to Granmarie, but doesn't touch her. He smiles ruefully. "I'm dead, Marie. You know that, and I know that."

She nods, hands covering her mouth, tears staining her cheeks. Her viola, solid and warm wood, lies on the stump beside the smaller, ghostly instrument belonging to her dead husband.

"But I'm here, like this, because of them." He gestures behind him, to the creatures beyond the doorway. Granmarie's eyes widen as she looks past him, and I realize that until this moment, she hasn't noticed anything or anyone but her lost love.

"Do you remember?" he asks her.

"My God," she whispers. "They were real. We played for the fairies. We really did."

"I suppose you could say they stole me. Just like the song." He smiles again, but then his face falls into sad lines. "That day, when — all I could think, as it was happening, was that I couldn't leave you behind.

I guess they heard me."

My mind reels. In Celtic lore, the fairy folk can steal souls of the dead before they leave for heaven. I don't remember why, but I do remember that much.

But I don't believe in heaven, or in souls…at least in the traditional sense.

Then again, I hadn't thought I believed in fairies, either.

"But when I called to you, you were gone," the ghost of my grandfather continues. "Nine years and I couldn't find you. Not until you started playing again."

My grandmother begins to sob.

I want to erase the guilt and sadness from her face. She couldn't have known. None of us could. It didn't — still doesn't — make any logical sense.

"There, lass," Duncan says. He reaches out, but he still can't touch her. "It came out all right in the end."

But has it come out all right?

What does any of this mean…for Granmarie, for us?

I clear my throat.

The ghost turns and sees me for the first time. A look of pure astonishment comes over his face, and he puts his hand to his heart. "Bless me! Is that our young Jessie? And playing a double bass, no less?"

He can't possibly be a false apparition created by fairy glamour, I decide. No one else has ever called me Jessie.

So what do you say to a ghost? "Hi, Grandpa Mac," is the best I can manage.

"Jess has been my rock," Granmarie says. "When I…heard you, and…somehow knew I would have to come back here, she was the one who offered to come with me. To help me when I needed it. And she's helped me every step of the way."

My cheeks warm with her praise. But now is when I should be

demanding answers from Duncan and the fairies. It's what a good granddaughter would do. I need to know what all of this means.

But Granmarie gets there first, her voice trembling again. "Duncan, what does this," she gestures to the doorway, the ring of watching creatures, the ghostly fiddle and her ghostly husband, "mean for us? What do you want? For me to —" her voice cracks on the words, "— to join you?"

Everything seems to hold its breath; I am forgotten once more.

"If I asked, would you?" His response is low and sad.

She hesitates, and her hands shake. I suddenly realize she did not ask the question out of fear.

It's longing that chokes her throat.

The knowledge hits me like a gut punch in slow motion. Would Granmarie really choose a life away from me, and the McAllister's, and living people who love her…if it meant she could be with her lost love?

And would she actually be choosing death, if she did?

I should speak.

I should tell her she can't leave.

That it wouldn't be fair to the rest of us.

I should tell her…

My left hand grips the fingerboard so hard that the strings feel like they're cutting into my fingers. I force myself to release it, to let the bass simply lean against me. It's a reminder: I'm supposed to be Granmarie's support.

I can't make an impossible choice for her, but perhaps I can help her find another way.

My specialty is solving problems, after all.

If Granmarie steps through that doorway, never to be seen again, it will be hell on the McAllister's. Search parties, inquiries, maybe suspicion of foul play. I'll be caught up in it too, and completely unable to tell the truth about it. And those are just the practical consequences, to say nothing of the emotional ones.

But if she doesn't go with Duncan, if she chooses the land of the living instead, can she go back to pretending everything was normal? Can she go back to America, all the while wondering what will happen when she dies someday…wondering if she will ever see him again?

Will she think to ask that question now, while she still can?

Granmarie still stands, silent, tears staining her cheeks.

I clear my throat again, feeling like an intruder. But I can't not know.

I just have to phrase this as neutrally as possible. "Grandpa Mac, what would have happened if Granmarie died without ever knowing about this? About you being here, with…them?"

They both turn to me, human and ghost, once again startled by my existence. The beings around me increase their barely-audible whispering and movement.

"Ah," Grandpa Mac says. He frowns, clearly unsure of why I'm asking. "Nothing good. I couldn't reach her without her heart being open. I couldn't even find her without the music. If she'd never heard me and never come here…" he pauses, searching for words. "The fairies wouldn't be able to do the same for her that they did for me."

My heart sinks.

But Granmarie speaks up, her face thoughtful. "But…Duncan, if I lived here, at the White Skye, would that be a different story? Could I live, and see you still, and then…when it's my time…" her voice trails off and she looks at him expectantly.

I hold my breath as Grandpa Mac listens to the whisperings through the archway.

His face clears, and, ghostly pale though he may be, breaks into one of his dazzling smiles. "Aye, that's it," he says. "If you live here with us — that is," his voice quiets so I can barely hear him, "if you choose it, the fairies can…ah…"

"Steal my soul when I die?" Granmarie's voice is soft too, but the corner of her mouth turns up, just a little. "Yes…I think I'd let them." Her voice grows stronger, warmer, and she moves to me, puts her arm around my shoulders. "But not a moment before my time, understand?"

She directs that to the beings around us.

I can't speak, my heart is so full.

This is the solution she needs, although it's not the one I want.

Keeping hold of the bass with one hand, I place the other over hers on my shoulder. "Thank you," I finally whisper, trying to ignore the small ache forming inside.

"No, thank you," she replies.

And thank the fairies, strange as it feels to think it. I don't know if their reasons are selfish or benevolent, but I'm not sure it matters. Marie and Duncan have a chance at a new adventure together, while still keeping the good things of this life, too.

I wanted to fix my grandmother's life, but this is like nothing I could have expected.

And Granmarie didn't need my help after all.

I leave them in the garden. They have so much between them. The connection has been made, and the decision, too. Now they just need time.

I close the gate and enter the ordered paths, blinking away the tears and taking deep breaths. It smells like growing things and earth here, and salt air, and a hint of rain.

The clouds are gathering again, as if they also know a resolution is at hand, and the strangeness of the weather — also a fairy device? — is no longer needed to show the way.

I realize now that ache I feel isn't just over the thought of leaving Granmarie in Skye. She won't be dead, she'll be with people she loves, she'll be happy. I'll still get to see her, at least once a year, if I can help it. There's the internet and phones, too.

But it won't be the same.

Maybe that's a good thing. Maybe I have spent too much time bending my life toward hers, putting my focus on my grandmother rather than my own life.

Neglecting things like my relationship with my mother.

Maybe when I go home in a week, when I leave Granmarie behind with her Duncan, I can start trying to mend things. I can take an active part in my family again, whether they think they want me or not.

After all, this has never been my story.

And while I have no regrets for my part in it, it's time for me to go out and create my own.

⌖ END ⌖

ACKNOWLEDGEMENTS

Of course this collection wouldn't exist without my mother, for many reasons, most of which I already gushed about in my introduction.

For every story I write, a huge portion of my thanks always has to go to Erik Kort, my husband and fellow writer. He gets me. He loves the weird, nerdy things I love. We make each other better: as writers, and as people.

And he also tromped all over Edinburgh's Royal Mile with me for a full day, so I could make notes on every single close, wynd, and court featured in "Sidewynd" and "The Flat Above the Wynd." Our feet and legs might have regretted it, but the rest of me did not. (Also huge gratitude to my marvelous sister Alyssa, who hosted us in Edinburgh at that time — during the final week of her dissertation, no less!)

I also have the bestselling authors Kristine Kathryn Rusch and Dean Wesley Smith to thank for their excellent writing workshops on the Oregon Coast. Three of the five stories in this collection got their start there, when I needed an outside hand to push me into finishing what I'd started. At one of their workshops I also made the acquaintance of writer Jamie Ferguson, who invited me to the 'Haunted' story bundle that spurred me to write "They Stole My Love Last Night."

People who spur me to write are always the best people. Thank all of you from the bottom of my heart.

Alexandra Brandt spent most of her childhood dressing up in fairy wings and parading in front of the mirror telling stories to herself. Not much has changed – she still loves a good costume, and tells herself stories every day. Her short stories appear in Fiction River and other anthologies. "We, the Ocean," her story in Fiction River's *No Humans Allowed* anthology, was described as "inventive, heartbreaking, and wholly original" by Hugo award-winning writer and editor Kristine Kathryn Rusch.

When not spinning tales, reading, or debating world-building details with her writer husband, Alex writes web copy and functions as a content marketer and graphic designer. She also dabbles in art, watches too many Sci-Fi TV shows, and welcomes any excuse to sit down and play tabletop games — from D&D to board games to cards. You can find her online:

www.alexandrajbrandt.com
Facebook: AlexandraBrandtWriter

www.ingramcontent.com/pod-product-compliance
Lightning Source LLC
Chambersburg PA
CBHW052009170626
46808CB00007B/2844